THE TRAVELS AND SURPRISING ADVENTURES OF BARON MUNCHAUSEN

RUDOLF ERICH RASPE (1736–1794) was born in Hanover, Germany of humble parentage. He studied natural sciences at the universities in Leipzig and Göttingen before becoming a university librarian and professor. He first gained fame for his poetry, translations, and scholarly papers, one of which Goethe called "a milestone of German science," and another of which led to his election to the Royal Society of London. His expertise in mineralogy also led to his appointment as curator of a gemstone collection held by the local count. But in 1775 he fled to England after it was discovered that he had been secretly selling the count's jewels to support his lavish lifestyle. In London he befriended many notables, including Benjamin Franklin and Horace Walpole . . . and continued to pursue schemes that often led to trouble, such as industrial spying in the nascent business of steam-engine manufacturing, and planting precious stones in supposed mineral fields he "discovered" and sold to speculators. He wrote *The Travels and Surprising Adventures of Baron Munchausen* in Cornwall, in the southwest of England, having moved there to pursue his geological research. It is presumed he had met the real-life Baron Munchausen (who lived in Göttingen), but the book would later be seen as less a (terribly) exaggerated portrait than a defiant spoof of the prevalent rationalism of the Enlightenment. Soon after its completion, however, Raspe was forced to flee to Scotland when it was discovered that he had fleeced another employer. He later moved to Ireland, where he died in Kilarney of typhoid.

D1262644

DAVID REES is a comedian and former political cartoonist whose books include *Get Your War On* and *How to Sharpen Pencils*.

THOMAS SECCOMBE (1866–1923) was a writer and assistant editor of the *Dictionary of National Biography*.

WILLIAM STRANG and **J.B. CLARK** were renowned artists who collaboratively illustrated *Sinbad the Sailor* and *Ali Baba and the Forty Thieves*. Strang was also a noted portraitist whose subjects included Thomas Hardy, Rudyard Kipling, and Vita Sackville-West.

THE NEVERSINK LIBRARY

I was by no means the only reader of books on board the Neversink. Several other sailors were diligent readers, though their studies did not lie in the way of belles-lettres. Their favourite authors were such as you may find at the book-stalls around Fulton Market; they were slightly physiological in their nature. My book experiences on board of the frigate proved an example of a fact which every book-lover must have experienced before me, namely, that though public libraries have an imposing air, and doubtless contain invaluable volumes, yet, somehow, the books that prove most agreeable, grateful, and companionable, are those we pick up by chance here and there; those which seem put into our hands by Providence; those which pretend to little, but abound in much. —HERMAN MELVILLE, WHITE JACKET

THE TRAVELS AND SURPRISING ADVENTURES OF BARON MUNCHAUSEN

RUDOLF ERICH RASPE

INTRODUCTION BY
DAVID REES

AFTERWORD BY
THOMAS SECCOMBE

ILLUSTRATED BY
WILLIAM STRANG AND J.B. CLARK

MELVILLE HOUSE PUBLISHING
BROOKLYN · LONDON

THE TRAVELS AND SURPRISING ADVENTURES
OF BARON MUNCHAUSEN

Originally published by Rudolf Erich Raspe, London, 1785; this edition is
based on the text published by Lawrence and Bullen, London, 1895

© Melville House 2012
Introduction © 2012, David Rees

Design by Christopher King

First Melville House printing: September 2012

Melville House Publishing
145 Plymouth Street
Brooklyn, NY 11201

www.mhpbooks.com

ISBN: 978-1-61219-123-2

Manufactured in the United States of America
1 2 3 4 5 6 7 8 9 10

Library of Congress Control Number: 2012947875

INTRODUCTION

BY DAVID REES

The book in your hands proves it's possible to be bludgeoned half to death by whimsy.

Readers who have never before encountered Baron Munchausen, or know him only from Terry Gilliam's 1988 film, may be surprised by the chaotic extent of his exploits—and the fathomless absurdity that serves as catalyst, obstacle, and handmaiden throughout this text.

The first item in Munchausen's extensive travelogue is the description of an elderly couple in a tree. (Why were they in a tree? They were harvesting cucumbers—"in this part of the globe that useful vegetable grows upon trees.") A terrible storm tosses the tree—and its occupants—high into the air. How high? I was expecting an answer of twenty feet or so. In fact, they were tossed "at least five miles above the earth." This is our first indication that the Baron's is not a typical itinerary.

The brief saga of the storm-tossed cucumber enthusiasts is perhaps the least outrageous event in the entire work, but it displays many of the qualities you will come to recognize as typical of the Baron's narrative:

unusual botany; extreme weather; a keen eye for the quantifiable ("considerably larger than twenty full-grown vultures;" "as near as I can calculate, I was near four hours and a half confined in the stomach of this animal").

And, of course: death. (When the cucumber tree falls back to earth it crushes a despot, upending the local political order.) Make no mistake: *The Travels and Surprising Adventures of Baron Munchausen* is a surprisingly violent book.

How violent? Animals are turned inside out (when they're not being cut in half); a man's decapitated head flies through the air, decapitating other men; a bridge of Munchausen's design is adorned with skulls; communities are decimated. *"When they all lay dead before me, I felt myself a second Samson, having slain my thousands."* According to my back-of-envelope calculations, the body count in this book is approximately fifty billion lives.

As he traipses from one catastrophe to the next, trailing clouds of gory as he comes, the Baron earns his place among other titans of fiction. About halfway through the *Surprising Adventures*—shortly after Munchausen grabs a bear's paws and simply waits for the creature to starve to death—I finally realized which classic character Munchausen most resembles, thanks to his omnipotence, the relentless forward thrust of his twin impulses to build and destroy, and the casual cruelty of his chaos-making: God. (*"[W]e saved as many of the white people as possible, but pushed all the blacks into the water again."*)

We rarely worry about Munchausen's fate: Even as he's fighting crocodiles, dispelling lions with loose gunpowder, or hitching a lift on the back of a drunk eagle, we trust in his capacity for the narrow escape and the eventual triumph. You may find yourself, in fact, vaguely resenting the good Baron for his invincibility, and wishing the stakes were a little higher for the man.

Perhaps it's best to think of Munchausen not as a protagonist in the traditional sense, but as the personification of a proactive psychological attitude. If, like me, you sometimes see the universe as a cheerless conspiracy to deny oneself peace of mind, you may take inspiration from the Baron's nonchalance and good humor even as he's sold into slavery, or confronted with vast islands of ice, or with a wolf chewing its way through the horse that leads his sled, or with Gog and Magog in the flesh.

Indeed, it's the Baron's sanguineness as much as the specifics of his adventures that lend this book so much of its strange charm, and we wonder how much of this charm was to be found in the original (that is, actual) Baron Munchausen. Is the man's personality refracted within these pages? It's hard to tell, as the particulars of *The Travels and Surprising Adventures of Baron Munchausen* are almost as surprising as the adventures themselves (see this edition's Afterword). The book's messy, peripatetic provenance recommended it to amendation, corruption, and confusion as authors piled on and scores of enthusiasts tried to make a little money off the good Baron's back.

Tall tales, like our merry baron, pay little heed to international borders; don't be surprised if some of the adventures recounted herein sound familiar. To take just one example: I first learned of the phenomenon of frozen speech—a musical equivalent is encountered by the Baron in Chapter VI—from the stories of Pecos Bill I read as a child. (Pecos Bill was the legendary American cowboy celebrated for lassoing a tornado—an exercise so culturally and meteorologically specific that one can almost forgive Munchausen for not attempting it himself.) Such is the genius of tall tales—like obscene playground rhymes and urban legends, the best ones sacrifice pedigree in favor of ubiquity, and become more powerful thereby.

A word of caution: As intimated above, this is not a book to be read in one sitting, or even in long stretches. The cacophony of destruction, the surreal lack of scale—not to mention the absence of any narrative logic—may fatigue even the hardiest of readers. The intensity of *The Surprising Adventures of Baron Munchausen* recommends that it be consumed in bursts. This is not consommé to be sipped in deference to its subtlety; it's tequila to be slammed, shot and shared with enthusiasm.

Did I mention the man can speak nine hundred and ninety-nine languages?

THE TRAVELS AND
SURPRISING ADVENTURES OF
BARON MUNCHAUSEN

TO THE PUBLIC.

HAVING heard, for the first time, that my adventures have been doubted and looked upon as jokes, I feel bound to come forward and vindicate my character for veracity, by paying three shillings at the Mansion House of this great city for the affidavits hereto appended.

This I have been forced into in regard of my own honour, although I have retired for many years from public and private life; and I hope that this, my last edition, will place me in a proper light with my readers.

AT THE CITY OF LONDON, ENGLAND.

We, the undersigned, as true believers in the *profit,* do most solemnly affirm, that all the adventures of our friend Baron Munchausen, in whatever country they may *lie,* are positive and simple facts. *And,* as we have been believed, whose adventures are tenfold more wonderful, so do we hope all true believers will give him their full faith and credence.

GULLIVER. ✕
SINBAD. ✕
ALADDIN. ✕

Sworn at the Mansion House
    9th Nov. last, in the absence
    of the Lord Mayor.
        JOHN *(the Porter)*

CONTENTS

CHAPTER I.

CHAPTER II.

CHAPTER III.

CHAPTER IV.

CHAPTER V.

CHAPTER VI.

CHAPTER VII.

CHAPTER VIII.

CHAPTER IX.

CHAPTER X.

CHAPTER XI.

CHAPTER XII.

The Frolic; its Consequences—Windsor Castle—St.
Paul's—College of Physicians, Undertakers, Sextons,
&c., almost ruined—Industry of the Apothecaries 58

CHAPTER XIII.

The Baron sails with Captain Phipps—Attacks two large
Bears, and has a very narrow Escape—Gains the Confidence of these Animals, and then destroys Thousands
of them; loads the Ship with their Hams and Skins;
makes Presents of the former, and obtains a general
Invitation to all City Feasts—A Dispute between the
Captain and the Baron, in which, from Motives of Politeness, the Captain is suffered to gain his Point—The
Baron declines the Honour of a Throne, and an Empress into the Bargain 60

CHAPTER XIV.

Our Baron excels Baron Tott beyond all Comparison, yet
fails in part of his Attempt—Gets into disgrace with
the Grand Seignior, who orders his Head to be cut
off—Escapes, and gets on board a vessel, in which he is
carried to Venice—Baron Tott's Origin, with some Account of that great man's Parents—Pope Ganganelli's
Amour—His Holiness fond of Shell-fish 66

CHAPTER XV.

A further Account of the journey from Harwich to Helvoetsluys—Description of a number of Marine Objects
never mentioned by any Traveller before—Rocks seen
in this Passage equal to the Alps in Magnitude; Lobsters, Crabs, &c., of an extraordinary Magnitude—A

CHAPTER XVI.

CHAPTER XVII.

CHAPTER XVIII.

CHAPTER XIX.

CHAPTER XX.

SUPPLEMENT.

CHAPTER XXI.

CHAPTER XXII.

CHAPTER XXIII.

CHAPTER XXIV.

CHAPTER XXV.

CHAPTER XXVI.

CHAPTER XXVII.

CHAPTER XXVIII.

CHAPTER XXIX.

CHAPTER XXX.

CHAPTER XXXI.

CHAPTER XXXII.

CHAPTER XXXIII.

CHAPTER XXXIV.

TRAVELS OF
BARON MUNCHAUSEN

CHAPTER I

[THE BARON IS SUPPOSED TO RELATE THESE
ADVENTURES TO HIS FRIENDS OVER A BOTTLE.]

*The Baron relates an account of his first travels—The aston-
ishing effects of a storm—Arrives at Ceylon; combats and
conquers two extraordinary opponents—Returns to Holland.*

SOME YEARS BEFORE MY BEARD ANNOUNCED
approaching manhood, or, in other words, when I was
neither man nor boy, but between both, I expressed in repeated conversations a strong desire of seeing the world,
from which I was discouraged by my parents, though my
father had been no inconsiderable traveller himself, as
will appear before I have reached the end of my singular, and, I may add, interesting adventures. A cousin, by
my mother's side, took a liking to me, often said I was a
fine forward youth, and was much inclined to gratify my

curiosity. His eloquence had more effect than mine, for my father consented to my accompanying him in a voyage to the island of Ceylon, where his uncle had resided as governor many years.

We sailed from Amsterdam with despatches from their High Mightinesses the States of Holland. The only circumstance which happened on our voyage worth relating was the wonderful effects of a storm, which had torn up by the roots a great number of trees of enormous bulk and height, in an island where we lay at anchor to take in wood and water; some of these trees weighed many tons, yet they were carried by the wind so amazingly high, that they appeared like the feathers of small birds floating in the air, for they were at least five miles above the earth: however, as soon as the storm subsided they all fell perpendicularly into their respective places, and took root again, except the largest, which happened, when it was blown into the air, to have a man and his wife, a very honest old couple, upon its branches, gathering cucumbers (in this part of the globe that useful vegetable grows upon trees): the weight of this couple, as the tree descended, over-balanced the trunk, and brought it down in an horizontal position: it fell upon the chief man of the island, and killed him on the spot; he had quitted his house in the storm, under an apprehension of its falling upon him, and was returning through his own garden when this fortunate accident happened. The word fortunate, here, requires some explanation. This chief was a man of a very avaricious and oppressive disposition, and though he had no family, the natives of the island were half-starved by his oppressive and infamous impositions.

The very goods which he had thus taken from them were spoiling in his stores, while the poor wretches from whom they were plundered were pining in poverty. Though the destruction of this tyrant was accidental, the people chose the cucumber-gatherers for their governors, as a mark of their gratitude for destroying, though accidentally, their late tyrant.

After we had repaired the damages we sustained in this remarkable storm, and taken leave of the new governor and his lady, we sailed with a fair wind for the object of our voyage.

In about six weeks we arrived at Ceylon, where we were received with great marks of friendship and true politeness. The following singular adventures may not prove unentertaining. After we had resided at Ceylon about a fortnight I accompanied one of the governor's brothers upon a shooting party. He was a strong, athletic man, and being used to that climate (for he had resided there some years), he bore the violent heat of the sun much better than I could; in our excursion he had made a considerable progress though a thick wood when I was only at the entrance.

Near the banks of a large piece of water, which had engaged my attention, I thought I heard a rustling noise behind; on turning about I was almost petrified (as who would not be?) at the sight of a lion, which was evidently approaching with the intention of satisfying his appetite with my poor carcase, and that without asking my consent. What was to be done in this horrible dilemma? I had not even a moment for reflection; my piece was only charged with swan-shot, and I had no other about me: however, though I could have no idea of killing such an

animal with that weak kind of ammunition, yet I had
some hopes of frightening him by the report, and perhaps of wounding him also. I immediately let fly, without
waiting till he was within reach, and the report did but
enrage him, for he now quickened his pace, and seemed
to approach me full speed: I attempted to escape, but that
only added (if an addition could be made) to my distress;
for the moment I turned about I found a large crocodile,
with his mouth extended almost ready to receive me. On
my right hand was the piece of water before mentioned,
and on my left a deep precipice, said to have, as I have
since learned, a receptacle at the bottom for venomous
creatures; in short I gave myself up as lost, for the lion
was now upon his hind-legs, just in the act of seizing me;
I fell involuntarily to the ground with fear, and, as it afterwards appeared, he sprang over me. I lay some time in
a situation which no language can describe, expecting to
feel his teeth or talons in some part of me every moment:
after waiting in this prostrate situation a few seconds I
heard a violent but unusual noise, different from any
sound that had ever before assailed my ears; nor is it at
all to be wondered at, when I inform you from whence
it proceeded: after listening for some time, I ventured to
raise my head and look round, when, to my unspeak-
able joy, I perceived the lion had, by the eagerness with
which he sprung at me, jumped forward, as I fell, into
the crocodile's mouth! which, as before observed, was
wide open; the head of the one stuck in the throat of the
other! and they were struggling to extricate themselves! I
fortunately recollected my *couteau de chasse*, which was
by my side; with this instrument I severed the lion's head
at one blow, and the body fell at my feet! I then, with the

butt-end of my fowling-piece, rammed the head farther into the throat of the crocodile, and destroyed him by suffocation, for he could neither gorge nor eject it.

Soon after I had thus gained a complete victory over my two powerful adversaries my companion arrived in search of me; for finding I did not follow him into the wood, he returned, apprehending I had lost my way, or met with some accident.

After mutual congratulations, we measured the crocodile, which was just forty feet in length.

As soon as we had related this extraordinary adventure to the governor, he sent a wagon and servants, who brought home the two carcases. The lion's skin was properly preserved, with its hair on, after which it was made into tobacco-pouches, and presented by me, upon our return to Holland, to the burgomasters, who, in return, requested my acceptance of a thousand ducats.

The skin of the crocodile was stuffed in the usual manner, and makes a capital article in their public museum at Amsterdam, where the exhibitor relates the whole story to each spectator, with such additions as he thinks proper. Some of his variations are rather extravagant; one of them is, that the lion jumped quite through the crocodile, and was making his escape at the back door, when, as soon as his head appeared, Monsieur the Great Baron (as he is pleased to call me) cut it off, and three feet of the crocodile's tail along with it; nay, so little attention has this fellow to the truth, that he sometimes adds, as soon as the crocodile missed his tail, he turned about, snatched the *couteau de chasse* out of Monsieur's hand, and swallowed it with such eagerness that it pierced his heart and killed him immediately!

The little regard which this impudent knave has to veracity makes me sometimes apprehensive that my *real facts* may fall under suspicion, by being found in company with his confounded inventions.

CHAPTER II

In which the Baron proves himself a good shot—He loses his horse, and finds a wolf—Makes him draw his sledge—Promises to entertain his company with a relation of such facts as are well deserving their notice.

I SET OFF FROM ROME ON A JOURNEY TO Russia, in the midst of winter, from a just notion that frost and snow must of course mend the roads, which every traveller had described as uncommonly bad through the northern parts of Germany, Poland, Courland, and Livonia. I went on horseback, as the most convenient manner of travelling; I was but lightly clothed, and of this I felt the inconvenience the more I advanced northeast. What must not a poor old man have suffered in that severe weather and climate, whom I saw on a bleak common in Poland, lying on the road, helpless, shivering, and hardly having wherewithal to cover his nakedness? I pitied the poor soul: though I felt the severity of the air myself, I threw my mantle over him, and immediately I heard a voice from the heavens, blessing me for that piece of charity, saying—

"You will be rewarded, my son, for this in time."

I went on: night and darkness overtook me. No village

was to be seen. The country was covered with snow, and I was unacquainted with the road.

Tired, I alighted, and fastened my horse to something like a pointed stump of a tree, which appeared above the snow; for the sake of safety I placed my pistols under my arm, and laid down on the snow, where I slept so soundly that I did not open my eyes till full daylight. It is not easy to conceive my astonishment to find myself in the midst of a village, lying in a churchyard; nor was my horse to be seen, but I heard him soon after neigh somewhere above me. On looking upwards I beheld him hanging by his bridle to the weather-cock of the steeple. Matters were now very plain to me: the village had been covered with snow overnight; a sudden change of weather had taken place; I had sunk down to the churchyard whilst asleep, gently, and in the same proportion as the snow had melted away; and what in the dark I had taken to be a stump of a little tree appearing above the snow, to which I had tied my horse, proved to have been the cross or weather-cock of the steeple!

Without long consideration I took one of my pistols, shot the bridle in two, brought down the horse, and proceeded on my journey. [Here the Baron seems to have forgot his feelings; he should certainly have ordered his horse a feed of corn, after fasting so long.]

He carried me well—advancing into the interior parts of Russia. I found travelling on horseback rather unfashionable in winter, therefore I submitted, as I always do, to the custom of the country, took a single horse sledge, and drove briskly towards St. Petersburg. I do not exactly recollect whether it was in Eastland or Jugemanland, but I remember that in the midst of a dreary forest I spied a terrible wolf making after me, with all the speed of ravenous winter hunger. He soon overtook me. There was no possibility of escape. Mechanically I laid myself down flat in the sledge, and let my horse run for our safety. What I wished, but hardly hoped or expected, happened immediately after. The wolf did not mind me in the least, but took a leap over me, and falling furiously on the horse, began instantly to tear and devour the hind-part of the poor animal, which ran the faster for his pain and terror. Thus unnoticed and safe myself, I lifted my head slyly up, and with horror I beheld that the wolf had ate his way into the horse's body; it was not long before he had fairly forced himself into it, when I took my advantage, and fell upon him with the butt-end of my whip. This unexpected attack in his rear frightened him so much, that he leaped forward with all his might: the horse's carcase dropped on the ground, but in his place the wolf was in the harness, and I on my part whipping him continually: we both arrived in full career safe to St. Petersburg, contrary to our respective expectations, and very much to the astonishment of the spectators.

I shall not tire you, gentlemen, with the politics, arts, sciences, and history of this magnificent metropolis of Russia, nor trouble you with the various intrigues and pleasant adventures I had in the politer circles of that country, where the lady of the house always receives the visitor with a dram and a salute. I shall confine myself rather to the greater and nobler objects of your attention, horses and dogs, my favourites in the brute creation; also to foxes, wolves, and bears, with which, and game in general, Russia abounds more than any other part of the world; and to such sports, manly exercises, and feats of gallantry and activity, as show the gentleman better than musty Greek or Latin, or all the perfume, finery, and capers of French wits or *petit-maîtres*.

CHAPTER III

An encounter between the Baron's nose and a door post, with its wonderful effects—Fifty brace of ducks and other fowl destroyed by one shot—Flogs a fox out of his skin—Leads an old sow home in a new way, and vanquishes a wild boar.

IT WAS SOME TIME BEFORE I COULD OBTAIN A commission in the army, and for several months I was perfectly at liberty to sport away my time and money in the most gentleman-like manner. You may easily imagine that I spent much of both out of town with such gallant fellows as knew how to make the most of an open forest country. The very recollection of those amusements gives me fresh spirits, and creates a warm wish for a repetition of them. One morning I saw, through the windows of my bed-room, that a large pond not far off was covered with wild ducks. In an instant I took my gun from the corner, ran down-stairs and out of the house in such a hurry, that I imprudently struck my face against the door-post. Fire flew out of my eyes, but it did not prevent my intention; I soon came within shot, when, levelling my piece, I observed to my sorrow, that even the flint had sprung from the cock by the violence of the shock I had just received. There was no time to be lost. I presently remembered the

effect it had on my eyes, therefore opened the pan, levelled my piece against the wild fowls, and my fist against
one of my eyes. [The Baron's eyes have retained fire ever
since, and appear particularly illuminated when he re-

lates this anecdote.] A hearty
blow drew sparks again; the
shot went off, and I killed
fifty brace of ducks, twenty
widgeons, and three couple
of teals. Presence of mind is
the soul of manly exercises.
If soldiers and sailors owe
to it many of their lucky escapes, hunters and sportsmen
are not less beholden to it for
many of their successes. In a
noble forest in Russia I met a
fine black fox, whose valuable
skin it would have been a pity
to tear by ball or shot. Reynard
stood close to a tree. In a twin-

kling I took out my ball, and placed a good spike-nail in
its room, fired, and hit him so cleverly that I nailed his
brush fast to the tree. I now went up to him, took out my
hanger, gave him a cross-cut over the face, laid hold of
my whip, and fairly flogged him out of his fine skin.

Chance and good luck often correct our mistakes; of
this I had a singular instance soon after, when, in the
depth of a forest, I saw a wild pig and sow running close
behind each other. My ball had missed them, yet the foremost pig only ran away, and the sow stood motionless,
as fixed to the ground. On examining into the matter,

I found the latter one to be an old sow, blind with age, which had taken hold of her pig's tail, in order to be led along by filial duty. My ball, having passed between the two, had cut his leading-string, which the old sow continued to hold in her mouth; and as her former guide did not draw her on any longer, she had stopped of course; I therefore laid hold of the remaining end of the pig's tail, and led the old beast home without any farther trouble on my part, and without any reluctance or apprehension on the part of the helpless old animal.

Terrible as these wild sows are, yet more fierce and dangerous are the boars, one of which I had once the misfortune to meet in a forest, unprepared for attack or defence. I retired behind an oak-tree just when the furious animal levelled a side-blow at me, with such force, that his tusks pierced through the tree, by which means he could neither repeat the blow nor retire. Ho, ho! thought I, I shall soon have you now! and immediately I laid hold of a stone, wherewith I hammered and bent his tusks in such a manner, that he could not retreat by any means, and must wait my return from the next village, whither I went for ropes and a cart, to secure him properly, and to carry him off safe and alive, in which I perfectly succeeded.

CHAPTER IV

Reflections on Saint Hubert's stag—Shoots a stag with cherry-stones; the wonderful effects of it—Kills a bear by extraordinary dexterity; his danger pathetically described—Attacked by a wolf, which he turns inside out—Is assailed by a mad dog, from which he escapes—The Baron's cloak seized with madness, by which his whole wardrobe is thrown into confusion.

YOU HAVE HEARD, I DARE SAY, OF THE HUNTER and sportsman's saint and protector, St. Hubert, and of the noble stag, which appeared to him in the forest, with the holy cross between his antlers. I have paid my homage to that saint every year in good fellowship, and seen this stag a thousand times, either painted in churches, or embroidered in the stars of his knights; so that, upon the honour and conscience of a good sportsman, I hardly know whether there may not have been formerly, or whether there are not such crossed stags even at this present day. But let me rather tell what I have seen myself: Having one day spent all my shot, I found myself unexpectedly in presence of a stately stag, looking at me as unconcernedly as if he had known of my empty pouches. I charged immediately with powder, and upon it a good handful of cherry-stones, for I had sucked the

17

fruit as far as the hurry would permit. Thus I let fly at him, and hit him just on the middle of the forehead, between his antlers; it stunned him—he staggered—yet he made off. A year or two after, being with a party in the same forest, I beheld a noble stag with a fine full grown cherry-tree above ten feet high between his antlers. I immediately recollected my former adventure, looked upon him as my property, and brought him to the ground by one shot, which at once gave me the haunch and cherry-sauce; for the tree was covered with the richest fruit, the like I had never tasted before. Who knows but some passionate holy sportsman, or sporting abbot or bishop, may have shot, planted, and fixed the cross between the antlers of St. Hubert's stag, in a manner similar to this? They always have been, and still are, famous for plantations of crosses and antlers; and in a case of distress or dilemma, which too often happens to keen sportsmen, one is apt to grasp at anything for safety, and to try any expedient rather than miss the favourable opportunity. I have many times found myself in that trying situation.

What do you say of this, for example? daylight and powder were spent one day in a Polish forest.
When I was going home a terrible bear made up to me in great speed, with open mouth, ready to fall upon me; all my pockets were searched in an instant for powder and ball, but in vain; I found nothing but two spare flints; one I flung with all my might into the monster's open jaws, down his throat. It gave him pain and made him turn about, so that I could level the second at his back-door, which, indeed, I did with wonderful success; for it flew in, met the first flint in the stomach, struck fire, and blew up the bear with a terrible explosion. Though I came safe

off that time, yet I should not wish to try it again, or venture against bears with no other ammunition.

There is a kind of fatality in it. The fiercest and most dangerous animals generally came upon me when defenceless, as if they had a notion or an instinctive intimation of it. Thus a frightful wolf rushed upon me so suddenly, and so close, that I could do nothing but follow mechanical instinct, and thrust my fist into his open mouth. For safety's sake I pushed on and on, till my arm was fairly in up to the shoulder. How should I disengage myself? I was not much pleased with my awkward situation—with a wolf face to face; our ogling was not of the most pleasant kind. If I withdrew my arm then the animal would fly the more furiously upon me; that I saw in his flaming eyes. In short, I laid hold of his tail, turned him inside out like a glove, and flung him to the ground, where I left him.

The same expedient would not have answered against a mad dog, which soon after came running against me in a narrow street at St. Petersburg. Run who can, I thought; and to do this the better, I threw off my fur cloak, and was safe within doors in an instant. I sent my servant for the cloak, and he put it in the wardrobe with my other clothes. The day after I was amazed and frightened by Jack's bawling, "For God's sake, sir, your fur cloak is mad!" I hastened up to him, and found almost all my clothes tossed about and torn to pieces. The fellow was perfectly right in his apprehensions about the fur cloak's madness. I saw him myself just then falling upon a fine full-dress suit, which he shook and tossed in an unmerciful manner.

CHAPTER V

The effects of great activity and presence of mind—A favourite hound described, which pups while pursuing a hare; the hare also litters while pursued by the hound—Presented with a famous horse by Count Przobossky, with which he performs many extraordinary feats.

ALL THESE NARROW AND LUCKY ESCAPES, gentlemen, were chances turned to advantage by presence of mind and vigorous exertions, which, taken together, as everybody knows, make the fortunate sportsman, sailor, and soldier; but he would be a very blamable and imprudent sportsman, admiral, or general, who would always depend upon chance and his stars, without troubling himself about those arts which are their particular pursuits, and without providing the very best implements, which insure success. I was not blamable either way; for I have always been as remarkable for the excellency of my horses, dogs, guns, and swords, as for the proper manner of using and managing them, so that upon the whole I may hope to be remembered in the forest, upon the turf, and in the field. I shall not enter here into any detail of my stables, kennel, or armoury; but a favourite bitch of mine I cannot help mentioning to you; she was

a greyhound; and I never had or saw a better. She grew old in my service, and was not remarkable for her size, but rather for her uncommon swiftness. I always coursed with her. Had you seen her you must have admired her, and would not have wondered at my predilection, and at my coursing her so much. She ran so fast, so much, and so long in my service, that she actually ran off her legs; so that, in the latter part of her life, I was under the necessity of working and using her only as a terrier, in which quality she still served me many years.

Coursing one day a hare, which appeared to me uncommonly big, I pitied my poor bitch, being big with pups, yet she would course as fast as ever. I could follow her on horseback only at a great distance. At once I heard a cry as it were of a pack of hounds —but so weak and faint that I hardly knew what to make of it. Coming up to them, I was greatly surprised. The hare had littered in running; the same had happened to my bitch in coursing, and there were just as many leverets as pups. By instinct the former ran, the latter coursed: and thus I found myself in possession at once of six hares, and as many dogs, at the end of a course which had only begun with one.

I remember this, my wonderful bitch, with the same pleasure and tenderness as a superb Lithuanian horse, which no money could have bought. He became mine by an accident, which gave me an opportunity of showing my horsemanship to a great advantage. I was at Count Przobossky's noble country-seat in Lithuania, and remained with the ladies at tea in the drawing-room, while the gentlemen were down in the yard, to see a young horse of blood which had just arrived from the stud. We suddenly heard a noise of distress; I hastened

down-stairs, and found the horse so unruly, that no-body durst approach or mount him. The most resolute horsemen stood dismayed and aghast; despondency was expressed in every countenance, when, in one leap, I was on his back, took him by surprise, and worked him quite into gentleness and obedience, with the best display of horsemanship I was master of. Fully to show this to the ladies, and save them unnecessary trouble, I forced him to leap in at one of the open windows of the tea-room, walked round several times, pace, trot, and gallop, and at last made him mount the tea-table, there to repeat his lessons in a pretty style of miniature which was exceedingly pleasing to the ladies, for he performed them amazingly well, and did not break either cup or saucer. It placed me so high in their opinion, and so well in that of the noble lord, that, with his usual politeness, he begged I would accept of this young horse, and ride him full career to conquest and honour in the campaign against the Turks, which was soon to be opened, under the command of Count Munich.

I could not indeed have received a more agreeable

present, nor a more ominous one at the opening of that campaign, in which I made my apprenticeship as a soldier. A horse so gentle, so spirited, and so fierce—at once a lamb and a Bucephalus, put me always in mind of the soldier's and the gentleman's duty! of young Alexander, and of the astonishing things he performed in the field.

We took the field, among several other reasons, it seems, with an intention to retrieve the character of the Russian arms, which had been blemished a little by Czar Peter's last campaign on the Pruth; and this we fully accomplished by several very fatiguing and glorious campaigns under the command of that great general I mentioned before.

Modesty forbids individuals to arrogate to themselves great successes or victories, the glory of which is generally engrossed by the commander—nay, which is rather awkward, by kings and queens who never smelt gunpowder but at the field-days and reviews of their troops; never saw a field of battle, or an enemy in battle array.

Nor do I claim any particular share of glory in the great engagements with the enemy. We all did our duty, which, in the patriot's, soldier's, and gentleman's language, is a very comprehensive word, of great honour, meaning, and import, and of which the generality of idle quidnuncs and coffee-house politicians can hardly form any but a very mean and contemptible idea. However, having had the command of a body of hussars, I went upon several expeditions, with discretionary powers; and the success I then met with is, I think, fairly and only to be placed to my account, and to that of the brave fellows whom I led on to conquest and to victory. We had very hot work once in the van of the army, when we

drove the Turks into Oczakow. My spirited Lithuanian
had almost brought me into a scrape: I had an advanced
fore-post, and saw the enemy coming against me in a
cloud of dust, which left me rather uncertain about their
actual numbers and real intentions: to wrap myself up
in a similar cloud was common prudence, but would
not have much advanced my knowledge, or answered
the end for which I had been sent out; therefore I let my
flankers on both wings spread to the right and left, and
make what dust they could, and I myself led on straight
upon the enemy, to have a nearer sight of them: in this
I was gratified, for they stood and fought, till, for fear of
my flankers, they began to move off rather disorderly.
This was the moment to fall upon them with spirit; we
broke them entirely—made a terrible havoc amongst
them, and drove them not only back to a walled town
in their rear, but even through it, contrary to our most
sanguine expectation.

The swiftness of my Lithuanian enabled me to be
foremost in the pursuit; and seeing the enemy fairly
flying through the opposite gate, I thought it would be
prudent to stop in the market-place, to order the men to
rendezvous. I stopped, gentlemen; but judge of my astonishment when in this market-place I saw not one of my
hussars about me! Are they scouring the other streets?
or what is become of them? They could not be far off,
and must, at all events, soon join me. In that expectation I walked my panting Lithuanian to a spring in this
market-place, and let him drink. He drank uncommonly,
with an eagerness not to be satisfied, but natural enough;
for when I looked round for my men, what should I see,
gentlemen! the hind part of the poor creature—croup

and legs were missing, as if he had been cut in two, and the water ran out as it came in, without refreshing or doing him any good! How it could have happened was quite a mystery to me, till I returned with him to the town-gate. There I saw, that when I rushed in pell-mell with the flying enemy, they had dropped the portcullis (a heavy falling door, with sharp spikes at the bottom, let down suddenly to prevent the entrance of an enemy into a fortified town) unperceived by me, which had totally cut off his hind part, that still lay quivering on the outside of the gate. It would have been an irreparable loss, had not our farrier contrived to bring both parts together while hot. He sewed them up with sprigs and young shoots of laurels that were at hand; the wound healed, and, what could not have happened but to so glorious a horse, the sprigs took root in his body, grew up, and formed a bower over me; so that afterwards I could go upon many other expeditions in the shade of my own and my horse's laurels.

CHAPTER VI

The Baron is made a prisoner of war, and sold for a slave—
Keeps the Sultan's bees, which are attacked by two bears—Loses
one of his bees; a silver hatchet, which he throws at the bears, re-
bounds and flies up to the moon; brings it back by an ingenious
invention; falls to the earth on his return, and helps himself out
of a pit—Extricates himself from a carriage which meets his in
a narrow road, in a manner never before attempted nor prac-
tised since—The wonderful effects of the frost upon his servant's
French horn.

I WAS NOT ALWAYS SUCCESSFUL. I HAD THE misfortune to be overpowered by numbers, to be made prisoner of war; and, what is worse, but always usual among the Turks, to be sold for a slave. [The Baron was afterwards in great favour with the Grand Seignior, as will appear hereafter.] In that state of humiliation my daily task was not very hard and laborious, but rather singular and irksome. It was to drive the Sultan's bees every morning to their pasture-grounds, to attend them all the day long, and against night to drive them back to their hives. One evening I missed a bee, and soon observed that two bears had fallen upon her to tear her to pieces for the honey she carried. I had nothing like an offensive weapon in my hands but the silver hatchet, which is the badge of the Sultan's gardeners and farmers. I threw it at the robbers, with an intention to frighten them away, and set the poor bee at liberty; but, by an unlucky turn of my arm, it flew upwards, and continued rising till it reached the moon. How should I recover it? how fetch it down again? I recollected that Turkey-beans grow very quick, and run up to an astonishing height. I planted one immediately; it grew, and actually fastened itself to one of the moon's horns. I had no more to do now but to climb up by it into the moon, where I safely arrived, and had a troublesome piece of business before I could find my silver hatchet, in a place where every thing has the brightness of silver; at last, however, I found it in a heap of chaff and chopped

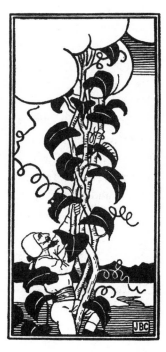

straw. I was now for returning: but, alas! the heat of the sun had dried up my bean; it was totally useless for my descent: so I fell to work, and twisted me a rope of that chopped straw, as long and as well as I could make it. This I fastened to one of the moon's horns, and slid down to the end of it. Here I held myself fast with the left hand, and with the hatchet in my right, I cut the long, now useless end of the upper part, which, when tied to the lower end, brought me a good deal lower: this repeated splicing and tying of the rope did not improve its quality, or bring me down to the Sultan's farm. I was four or five miles from the earth at least when it broke; I fell to the ground with such amazing violence, that I found myself stunned, and in a hole nine fathoms deep at least, made by the weight of my body falling from so great a height: I recovered, but knew not how to get out again; however, I dug slopes or steps with my finger-nails (the Baron's nails were then of forty years' growth), and easily accomplished it.

Peace was soon after concluded with the Turks, and gaining my liberty, I left St. Petersburg at the time of that singular revolution, when the emperor in his cradle, his mother, the Duke of Brunswick, her father, Field-Marshal Munich, and many others were sent to Siberia. The winter was then so uncommonly severe all over Europe, that ever since the sun seems to be frost-bitten. At my return to this place, I felt on the road greater inconveniences than those I had experienced on my setting out.

I travelled post, and finding myself in a narrow lane, bid the postillion give a signal with his horn, that other travellers might not meet us in the narrow passage. He blew with all his might; but his endeavours were in vain, he could not make the horn sound, which was unaccountable, and rather unfortunate, for soon after we found ourselves in the presence of another coach coming the other way: there was no proceeding; however, I got out of my carriage, and being pretty strong, placed it, wheels and all, upon my head: I then jumped over a hedge about nine feet high (which, considering

the weight of the coach, was rather difficult) into a field, and came out again by another jump into the road beyond the other carriage: I then went back for the horses, and placing one upon my head, and the other under my left arm, by the same means brought them to my coach, put to, and proceeded to an inn at the end of our stage. I should have told you that the horse under my arm was very spirited, and not above four years old; in making my second spring over the hedge, he expressed great dislike to that violent kind of motion by kicking and snorting; however, I confined his hind legs by putting them into my coat-pocket. After we arrived at the inn my postillion and I refreshed ourselves: he hung his horn on a peg near the kitchen fire; I sat on the other side.

Suddenly we heard a *tereng! tereng! teng! teng!* We looked round, and now found the reason why the postillion had not been able to sound his horn; his tunes were frozen up in the horn, and came out now by thawing, plain enough, and much to the credit of the driver, so that the honest fellow entertained us for some time with a variety of tunes, without putting his mouth to the horn—"The King of Prussia's March," "Over the Hill and over the Dale," with many other favourite tunes; at length the thawing entertainment concluded, as I shall this short account of my Russian travels.

Some travellers are apt to advance more than is perhaps strictly true; if any of the company entertain a doubt of my veracity, I shall only say to such, I pity their want of faith, and must request they will take leave before I begin the second part of my adventures, which are as strictly founded in fact as those I have already related.

CHAPTER VII

The Baron relates his adventures on a voyage to North America, which are well worth the reader's attention—Pranks of a whale—A sea-gull saves a sailor's life—The Baron's head forced into his stomach—A dangerous leak stopped à posteriori.

I EMBARKED AT PORTSMOUTH IN A FIRST-RATE English man-of-war, of one hundred guns, and fourteen hundred men, for North America. Nothing worth relating happened till we arrived within three hundred leagues of the river St. Laurence, when the ship struck with amazing force against (as we supposed) a rock; however, upon heaving the lead we could find no bottom, even with three hundred fathom. What made this circumstance the more wonderful, and indeed beyond all comprehension, was, that the violence of the shock was such that we lost our rudder, broke our bowsprit in the middle, and split all our masts from top to bottom, two of which went by the board; a poor fellow, who was aloft furling the main-sheet, was flung at least three leagues from the ship; but he fortunately saved his life by laying hold of the tail of a large sea-gull, who brought him back, and lodged him on the very spot from whence he was thrown. Another proof of the violence of the shock

was the force with which the people between decks were
driven against the floors above them; my head particularly was pressed into my stomach, where it continued
some months before it recovered its natural situation.
Whilst we were all in a state of astonishment at the general and unaccountable confusion in which we were
involved, the whole was suddenly explained by the appearance of a large whale, who had been basking, asleep,
within sixteen feet of the surface of the water. This animal
was so much displeased with the disturbance which our
ship had given him—for in our passage we had with our
rudder scratched his nose—that he beat in all the gallery
and part of the quarter-deck with his tail, and almost at
the same instant took the mainsheet anchor, which was
suspended, as it usually is, from the head, between his
teeth, and ran away with the ship, at least sixty leagues,
at the rate of twelve leagues an hour, when fortunately
the cable broke, and we lost both the whale and the anchor. However, upon our return to Europe, some months
after, we found the same whale within a few leagues of
the same spot, floating dead upon the water; it measured
above half a mile in length. As we could take but a small
quantity of such a monstrous animal on board, we got
our boats out, and with much difficulty cut off his head,
where, to our great joy, we found the anchor, and above
forty fathom of the cable, concealed on the left side of his
mouth, just under his tongue. [Perhaps this was the cause
of his death, as that side of his tongue was much swelled,
with a great degree of inflammation.] This was the only
extraordinary circumstance that happened on this voyage. One part of our distress, however, I had like to have
forgot: while the whale was running away with the ship

she sprung a leak, and the water poured in so fast, that all our pumps could not keep us from sinking; it was, however, my good fortune to discover it first. I found it a large hole about a foot diameter; you will naturally suppose this circumstance gives me infinite pleasure, when I inform you that this noble vessel was preserved, with all its crew, by a most fortunate thought! in short, I sat down over it, and could have dispensed with it had it been larger; nor will you be surprised when I inform you I am descended from Dutch parents. [The Baron's ancestors have but lately settled there; in another part of his adventures he boasts of royal blood.]

My situation, while I sat there, was rather cool, but the carpenter's art soon relieved me.

CHAPTER VIII

Bathes in the Mediterranean—Meets an unexpected companion—Arrives unintentionally in the regions of heat and darkness, from which he is extricated by dancing a hornpipe—Frightens his deliverers, and returns on shore.

I WAS ONCE IN GREAT DANGER OF BEING LOST in a most singular manner in the Mediterranean: I was bathing in that pleasant sea near Marseilles one summer's afternoon, when I discovered a very large fish, with his jaws quite extended, approaching me with the greatest velocity; there was no time to be lost, nor could I possibly avoid him. I immediately reduced myself to as small a size as possible, by closing my feet and placing my hands also near my sides, in which position I passed directly between his jaws, and into his stomach, where I remained some time in total darkness, and comfortably warm, as you may imagine; at last it occurred to me, that by giving him pain he would be glad to get rid of me: as I had plenty of room, I played my pranks, such as tumbling, hop, step, and jump, &c., but nothing seemed to disturb him so much as the quick motion of my feet in attempting to dance a hornpipe; soon after I began he put me out by sudden fits and starts: I persevered; at last he roared horridly, and stood up almost perpendicularly in the water, with his head and shoulders exposed, by which he was discovered by the people on board an Italian trader, then sailing by, who harpooned him in a few minutes. As soon as he was brought on board I heard the crew consulting how they should cut him up, so as to preserve the greatest quantity of oil. As I understood Italian, I was in most dreadful apprehensions lest their weapons employed in this business should destroy me also; therefore I stood as near the centre as possible, for there was room enough for a dozen men in this creature's stomach, and I naturally imagined they would begin with the extremities: however, my fears were soon dispersed, for they began by opening the bottom of the belly. As soon as I perceived a glimmering of light I called out lustily to be released from a situation in which I was now almost suffocated. It is impossible for me to do justice to the degree and kind of astonishment which sat upon every countenance at hearing a human voice issue from a fish, but more so at seeing a naked man walk upright out of his body; in short, gentlemen, I told them the whole story, as I have done you, whilst amazement struck them dumb.

After taking some refreshment, and jumping into the sea to cleanse myself, I swam to my clothes, which lay where I had left them on the shore. As near as I can calculate, I was near four hours and a half confined in the stomach of this animal.

CHAPTER IX

Adventures in Turkey, and upon the river Nile—Sees a balloon over Constantinople; shoots at, and brings it down; finds a French experimental philosopher suspended from it —Goes on an embassy to Grand Cairo, and returns upon the Nile, where he is thrown into an unexpected situation, and detained six weeks.

WHEN I WAS IN THE SERVICE OF THE TURKS I frequently amused myself in a pleasure-barge on the Marmora, which commands a view of the whole city of Constantinople, including the Grand Seignior's Seraglio. One morning, as I was admiring the beauty and serenity of the sky, I observed a globular substance in the air, which appeared to be about the size of a twelve-inch globe, with somewhat suspended from it. I immediately took up my largest and longest barrel fowling-piece, which I never travel or make even an excursion without, if I can help it; I charged with a ball, and fired at the globe, but to no purpose, the object being at too great a distance. I then put in a double quantity of powder, and five or six balls: this second attempt succeeded; all the balls took effect, and tore one side open, and brought it down. Judge my surprise when a most elegant gilt car, with a man in it, and part of a sheep which seemed to have been roasted, fell within two yards of me; when my astonishment had in some degree subsided, I ordered my people to row close to this strange aerial traveller.

I took him on board my barge (he was a native of France): he was much indisposed from his sudden fall into the sea, and incapable of speaking; after some time, however, he recovered, and gave the following account of himself, viz.: "About seven or eight days since, I cannot tell which, for I have lost my reckoning, having been most of the time where the sun never sets, I ascended from the Land's End in Cornwall, in the island of Great Britain, in the car from which I have been just taken, suspended from a very large balloon, and took a sheep with me, to try atmospheric experiments upon: unfortunately, the wind changed within ten minutes after my ascent, and instead of driving towards Exeter, where I intended to land, I was driven towards the sea, over which I suppose I have continued ever since, but much too high to make observations.

"The calls of hunger were so pressing, that the intended experiments upon heat and respiration gave way to them. I was obliged, on the third day, to kill the sheep for food; and being at that time infinitely above the moon, and for upwards of sixteen hours after so very near the sun that it scorched my eyebrows, I placed the carcase, taking care to skin it first, in that part of the car where the sun had sufficient power, or, in other words, where the balloon did not shade it from the sun, by which method it was well roasted in about two hours. This has been my food ever since." Here he paused, and seemed lost in viewing the objects about him. When I told him the buildings before us were the Grand Seignior's Seraglio at Constantinople, he seemed exceedingly affected, as he had supposed himself in a very different situation. "The cause," added he, "of my long flight, was owing to the failure of a string which was fixed to a valve in the balloon, intended to let out the inflammable air; and if it had not been fired at, and rent in the manner before mentioned, I might, like Mahomet, have been suspended between heaven and earth till doomsday."

The Grand Seignior, to whom I was introduced by the Imperial, Russian, and French ambassadors, employed me to negotiate a matter of great importance at Grand Cairo, and which was of such a nature that it must ever remain a secret.

I went there in great state by land; where, having completed the business, I dismissed almost all my attendants,
and returned like a private gentleman: the weather was
delightful, and that famous river the Nile was beautiful
beyond all description; in short, I was tempted to hire
a barge to descend by water to Alexandria. On the third
day of my voyage the river began to rise most amazingly
(you have all heard, I presume, of the annual overflow-
ing of the Nile), and on the next day it spread the whole
country for many leagues on each side! On the fifth, at
sunrise, my barge became entangled with what I at first
took for shrubs, but as the light became stronger I found
myself surrounded by almonds, which were perfectly
ripe, and in the highest perfection. Upon plumbing with
a line my people found we were at least sixty feet from
the ground, and unable to advance or retreat. At about
eight or nine o'clock, as near as I could judge by the alti-
tude of the sun, the wind rose suddenly, and canted our
barge on one side: here she filled, and I saw no more of
her for some time. Fortunately we all saved ourselves (six
men and two boys) by clinging to the tree, the boughs of
which were equal to our weight, though not to that of the
barge: in this situation we continued six weeks and three
days, living upon the almonds; I need not inform you
we had plenty of water. On the forty-second day of our
distress the water fell as rapidly as it had risen, and on
the forty-sixth we were able to venture down upon *terra
firma*. Our barge was the first pleasing object we saw,
about two hundred yards from the spot where she sunk.
After drying everything that was useful by the heat of
the sun, and loading ourselves with necessaries from the
stores on board, we set out to recover our lost ground,

and found, by the nearest calculation, we had been carried over garden-walls, and a variety of enclosures, above one hundred and fifty miles. In four days, after a very

tiresome journey on foot, with thin shoes, we reached the river, which was now confined to its banks, related our adventures to a boy, who kindly accommodated all our wants, and sent us forward in a barge of his own. In six days more we arrived at Alexandria, where we took shipping for Constantinople. I was received kindly by the grand Seignior, and had the honour of seeing the Seraglio, to which his highness introduced me himself.

CHAPTER X

Pays a visit during the siege of Gibraltar to his old friend General Elliot—Sinks a Spanish man-of-war—Wakes an old woman on the African coast—Destroys all the enemy's cannon; frightens the Count d'Artois, and sends him to Paris—Saves the lives of two English spies with the identical sling that killed Goliah; and raises the siege.

DURING THE LATE SIEGE OF GIBRALTAR I WENT with a provision-fleet, under Lord Rodney's command, to see my old friend General Elliot, who has, by his distinguished defence of that place, acquired laurels that can never fade. After the usual joy which generally attends the meeting of old friends had subsided, I went to examine the state of the garrison, and view the operations of the enemy, for which purpose the General accompanied me. I had brought a most excellent refracting telescope with me from London, purchased of Dollond, by the help of which I found the enemy were going to discharge a thirty-six pounder at the spot where we stood. I told the General what they were about; he looked through the glass also, and found my conjectures right. I immediately, by his permission, ordered a forty-eight pounder to be brought from a neighbouring battery, which I placed with so much exactness (having long studied the art of gunnery) that I was sure of my mark.

I continued watching the enemy till I saw the match placed at the touch-hole of their piece; at that very instant I gave the signal for our gun to be fired also.

About midway between the two pieces of cannon the balls struck each other with amazing force, and the effect was astonishing! The enemy's ball recoiled back with such violence as to kill the man who had discharged it, by carrying his head fairly off, with sixteen others which it met with in its progress to the Barbary coast, where its force, after passing through three masts of vessels that then lay in a line behind each other in the harbour, was so much spent, that it only broke its way through the

roof of a poor labourer's hut, about two hundred yards
inland, and destroyed a few teeth an old woman had left,
who lay asleep upon her back with her mouth open. The
ball lodged in her throat. Her husband soon after came
home, and endeavoured to extract it; but finding that im-
practicable, by the assistance of a rammer he forced it
into her stomach. Our ball did excellent service; for it
not only repelled the other in the manner just described,
but, proceeding as I intended it should, it dismounted
the very piece of cannon that had just been employed
against us, and forced it into the hold of the ship, where
it fell with so much force as to break its way through
the bottom. The ship immediately filled and sank, with
above a thousand Spanish sailors on board, besides a
considerable number of soldiers. This, to be sure, was a
most extraordinary exploit; I will not, however, take the
whole merit to myself; my judgment was the principal
engine, but chance assisted me a little; for I afterwards
found, that the man who charged our forty-eight ponder
put in, by mistake, a double quantity of powder, else we
could never have succeeded so much beyond all expectation, especially in repelling the enemy's ball.

General Elliot would have given me a commission for
this singular piece of service; but I declined everything,
except his thanks, which I received at a crowded table of
officers at supper on the evening of that very day.

As I am very partial to the English, who are beyond
all doubt a brave people, I determined not to take my
leave of the garrison till I had rendered them another
piece of service, and in about three weeks an opportunity
presented itself. I dressed myself in the habit of a *Popish
priest*, and at about one o'clock in the morning stole out of

the garrison, passed the enemy's lines, and arrived in the middle of their camp, where I entered the tent in which the Prince d'Artois was, with the commander-in-chief, and several other officers, in deep council, concerting a plan to storm the garrison next morning. My disguise was my protection; they suffered me to continue there, hearing everything that passed, till they went to their several beds. When I found the whole camp, and even the sentinels, were wrapped up in the arms of Morpheus, I began my work, which was that of dismounting all their cannon (above three hundred pieces), from forty-eight to twenty-four pounders, and throwing them three leagues into the sea. Having no assistance, I found this the hardest task I ever undertook, except swimming to the opposite shore with the famous Turkish piece of ordnance, described by Baron de Tott in his Memoirs, which I shall hereafter mention. I then piled all the carriages together in the centre of the camp, which, to prevent the noise of the wheels being heard, I carried in pairs under my arms; and a noble appearance they made, as high at least as the rock of Gibraltar. I then lighted a match by striking a flint stone, situated twenty feet from the ground (in an old wall built by the Moors when they invaded Spain), with the breech of an iron eight-and-forty pounder, and so set fire to the whole pile. I forgot to inform you that I threw all their ammunition-waggons upon the top.

Before I applied the lighted match I had laid the combustibles at the bottom so judiciously, that the whole was in a blaze in a moment. To prevent suspicion I was one of the first to express my surprise. The whole camp was, as you may imagine, petrified with astonishment: the general conclusion was, that their sentinels had been

bribed, and that seven or eight regiments of the garrison had been employed in this horrid destruction of
their artillery. Mr. Drinkwater, in his account of this famous siege, mentions the enemy sustaining a great loss
by a fire which happened in their camp, but never knew
the cause; how should he? as I never divulged it before
(though I alone saved Gibraltar by this night's business),
not even to General Elliot. The Count d'Artois and all his
attendants ran away in their fright, and never stopped on
the road till they reached Paris, which they did in about
a fortnight; this dreadful conflagration had such an effect
upon them that they were incapable of taking the least
refreshment for three months after, but, chameleon-like,
lived upon the air.

*If any gentleman will say he doubts the truth of this
story, I will fine him a gallon of brandy and make him
drink it at one draught.*

About two months after I had done the besieged this
service, one morning, as I sat at breakfast with General
Elliot, a shell (for I had not time to destroy their mortars
as well as their cannon) entered the apartment we were
sitting in; it lodged upon our table: the General, as most
men would do, quitted the room directly; but I took it up
before it burst, and carried it to top of the rock, when,
looking over the enemy's camp, on an eminence near the
sea-coast I observed a considerable number of people,
but could not, with my naked eye, discover how they
were employed. I had recourse again to my telescope,
when I found that two of our officers, one a general, the
other a colonel, with whom I had spent the preceding

evening, and who went out into the enemy's camp about midnight as spies, were taken, and then were actually going to be executed on a gibbet. I found the distance too great to throw the shell with my hand, but most fortunately recollecting that I had the very sling in my pocket which assisted David in slaying Goliah, I placed the shell in it, and immediately threw it in the midst of them: it burst as it fell, and destroyed all present, except the two culprits, who were saved by being suspended so high, for they were just turned off: however, one of the pieces of the shell fled with such force against the foot of the gibbet, that it immediately brought it down. Our two friends no sooner felt *terra firma* than they looked about for the cause; and finding their guards, executioner, and all, had taken it in their heads to die first, they directly extricated each other from their disgraceful cords, and then ran down to the sea-shore, seized a Spanish boat with two men in it, and made them row to one of our ships, which they did with great safety, and in a few minutes after, when I was relating to General Elliot how I had acted, they both took us by the hand, and after mutual congratulations we retired to spend the day with festivity.

CHAPTER XI

An interesting account of the Baron's ancestors—A quarrel relative to the spot where Noah built his ark—The history of the sling, and its properties—A favourite poet introduced upon no very reputable occasion—Queen Elizabeth's abstinence—The Baron's father crosses from England to Holland upon a marine horse, which he sells for seven hundred ducats.

YOU WISH (I CAN SEE BY YOUR COUNTENANCES) I would inform you how I became possessed of such a treasure as the sling just mentioned. (Here facts must be held sacred.) Thus then it was: I am a descendant of the wife of Uriah, whom we all know David was intimate with; she had several children by his majesty; they quarrelled once upon a matter of the first consequence, viz., the spot where Noah's ark was built, and where it rested after the flood. A separation consequently ensued. She had often heard him speak of this sling as his most valuable treasure: this she stole the night they parted; it was missed before she got out of his dominions, and she was pursued by no less than six of the king's body-guards: however, by using it herself she hit the first of them (for one was more active in the pursuit than the rest) where David did Goliah, and killed him on the spot. His companions were so alarmed at his fall that they retired, and

W.S.

left Uriah's wife to pursue her journey. She took with her, I should have informed you before, her favourite son by this connection, to whom she bequeathed the sling; and thus it has, without interruption, descended from father to son till it came into my possession. One of its possessors, my great-great-great-grandfather, who lived about two hundred and fifty years ago, was upon a visit to England, and became intimate with a poet who was a great deer-stealer; I think his name was Shakespeare: he frequently borrowed this sling, and with it killed so much of Sir Thomas Lucy's venison, that he narrowly escaped the fate of my two friends at Gibraltar. Poor Shakespeare was imprisoned, and my ancestor obtained his freedom in a very singular manner. Queen Elizabeth was then on the throne, but grown so indolent, that every trifling matter was become a trouble to her; dressing, undressing, eating, drinking, and some other offices which shall be nameless, made life a burden to her; all these things he enabled her to do without, or by a deputy! and what do you think was the only return she could prevail upon him to accept for such eminent services? setting Shakespeare at liberty! Such was his affection for that famous writer, that he would have shortened his own days to add to the number of his friend's.

I do not hear that any of the queen's subjects, particularly the *beef-eaters*, as they are vulgarly called to this day, however they might be struck with the novelty at the time, much approved of her living totally without food. She did not survive the practice herself above seven years and a half.

My father, who was the immediate possessor of this sling before me, told me the following anecdote:—

He was walking by the sea-shore at Harwich, with this sling in his pocket; before his paces had covered a mile he was attacked by a fierce animal called a seahorse, open-mouthed, who ran at him with great fury; he hesitated a moment, then took out his sling, retreated back about a hundred yards, stooped for a couple of pebbles, of which there were plenty under his feet, and slung them both so dexterously at the animal, that each stone put out an eye, and lodged in the cavities which their removal had occasioned. He now got upon his back, and drove him into the sea; for the moment he lost his sight he lost also his ferocity, and became as tame as possible: the sling was placed as a bridle in his mouth; he was guided with the greatest facility across the ocean, and in less than three hours they both arrived on the opposite shore, which is about thirty leagues. The master of the *Three Cups*, at Helvoetsluys, in Holland, purchased this marine horse, to make an exhibition of, for seven hundred ducats, which was upwards of three hundred pounds, and the next day my father paid his passage back in the packet to Harwich.

— *My father made several curious observations in this passage, which I will relate hereafter.*

CHAPTER XII

The frolic; its consequences—Windsor Castle—St. Paul's—
College of Physicians—Undertakers, sextons, &c., almost
ruined—Industry of the apothecaries.

THE FROLIC.

THIS FAMOUS SLING MAKES THE POSSESSOR
equal to any task he is desirous of performing.

I made a balloon of such extensive dimensions, that
an account of the silk it contained would exceed all credi-
bility; every mercer's shop and weaver's stock in London,
Westminster, and Spitalfields contributed to it: with this
balloon and my sling I played many tricks, such as taking one house from its station, and placing another in
its stead, without disturbing the inhabitants, who were
generally asleep, or too much employed to observe the
peregrinations of their habitations. When the sentinel at
Windsor Castle heard St. Paul's clock strike thirteen, it
was through my dexterity; I brought the buildings nearly
together that night, by placing the castle in St. George's
Fields, and carried it back again before daylight, without
waking any of the inhabitants; notwithstanding these exploits, I should have kept my balloon and its properties

a secret, if Montgolfier had not made the art of flying so public.

On the 30th of September, when the College of Physicians chose their annual officers, and dined sumptuously together, I filled my balloon, brought it over the dome of their building, clapped the sling round the golden ball at the top, fastening the other end of it to the balloon, and immediately ascended with the whole college to an immense height, where I kept them upwards of three months. You will naturally inquire what they did for food such a length of time? To this I answer, Had I kept them suspended twice the time, they would have experienced no inconvenience on that account, so amply, or rather extravagantly, had they spread their table for that day's feasting.

Though this was meant as an innocent frolic, it was productive of much mischief to several respectable characters amongst the clergy, undertakers, sextons, and grave-diggers: they were, it must be acknowledged, sufferers; for it is a well-known fact, that during the three months the college was suspended in the air, and therefore incapable of attending their patients, no deaths happened, except a few who fell before the scythe of Father Time, and some melancholy objects who, perhaps to avoid some trifling inconvenience here, laid the hands of violence upon themselves, and plunged into misery infinitely greater than that which they hoped by such a rash step to avoid, without a moment's consideration.

If the apothecaries had not been very active during the above time, half the undertakers in all probability would have been bankrupts.

CHAPTER XIII

A TRIP TO THE NORTH

The Baron sails with Captain Phipps, attacks two large bears, and has a very narrow escape—Gains the confidence of these animals, and then destroys thousands of them; loads the ship with their hams and skins; makes presents of the former, and obtains a general invitation to all city feasts—A dispute between the Captain and the Baron, in which, from motives of politeness, the Captain is suffered to gain his point—The Baron declines the honour of a throne, and an empress into the bargain.

WE ALL REMEMBER CAPTAIN PHIPPS'S (NOW Lord Mulgrave) last voyage of discovery to the north. I accompanied the captain, not as an officer, but a private friend. When we arrived in a high northern latitude I was viewing the objects around me with the telescope which I introduced to your notice in my Gibraltar adventures. I thought I saw two large white bears in violent action upon a body of ice considerably above the masts, and about half a league distance. I immediately took my carbine, slung it across my shoulder, and ascended the ice.

When I arrived at the top, the unevenness of the surface
made my approach to those animals troublesome and
hazardous beyond expression: sometimes hideous cavities opposed me, which I was obliged to spring over; in
other parts the surface was as smooth as a mirror, and
I was continually falling: as I approached near enough
to reach them, I found they were only at play. I immediately began to calculate the value of their skins, for
they were each as large as a well-fed ox: unfortunately,
at the very instant I was presenting my carbine my right
foot slipped, I fell upon my back, and the violence of the
blow deprived me totally of my senses for nearly half an
hour; however, when I recovered, judge of my surprise
at finding one of those large animals I have been just
describing had turned me upon my face, and was just
laying hold of the waistband of my breeches, which were
then new and made of leather: he was certainly going to
carry me feet foremost, God knows where, when I took
this knife (showing a large clasp knife) out of my side-
pocket, made a chop at one of his hind feet, and cut off
three of his toes; he immediately let me drop and roared
most horridly. I took up my carbine and fired at him as
he ran off; he fell directly. The noise of the piece roused
several thousands of these white bears, who were asleep
upon the ice within half a mile of me; they came immediately to the spot. There was no time to be lost. A most
fortunate thought arrived in my pericranium just at that
instant. I took off the skin and head of the dead bear in
half the time that some people would be in skinning a
rabbit, and wrapped myself in it, placing my own head
directly under Bruin's; the whole herd came round me
immediately, and my apprehensions threw me into a

most piteous situation to be sure: however, my scheme
turned out a most admirable one for my own safety. They
all came smelling, and evidently took me for a brother
Bruin; I wanted nothing but bulk to make an excellent
counterfeit: however, I saw several cubs amongst them
not much larger than myself. After they had all smelt me,
and the body of their deceased companion, whose skin
was now become my protector, we seemed very sociable,
and I found I could mimic all their actions tolerably well;
but at growling, roaring, and hugging they were quite
my masters. I began now to think how I might turn the
general confidence which I had created amongst these
animals to my advantage.

I had heard an old army surgeon say a wound in the
spine was instant death. I now determined to try the
experiment, and had again recourse to my knife, with
which I struck the largest in the back of the neck, near
the shoulders, but under great apprehensions, not doubt-
ing but the creature would, if he survived the stab, tear
me to pieces. However, I was remarkably fortunate, for
he fell dead at my feet without making the least noise.
I was now resolved to demolish them every one in the
same manner, which I accomplished without the least
difficulty; for although they saw their companions fall,
they had no suspicion of either the cause or the effect.
When they all lay dead before me, I felt myself a second
Samson, having slain my thousands.

To make short of the story, I went back to the ship,
and borrowed three parts of the crew to assist me in skinning them, and carrying the hams on board, which we
did in a few hours, and loaded the ship with them. As to
the other parts of the animals, they were thrown into the

sea, though I doubt not but the whole would eat as well as the legs, were they properly cured.

As soon as we returned I sent some of the hams, in the captain's name, to the Lords of the Admiralty, others to the Lords of the Treasury, some to the Lord Mayor and Corporation of London, a few to each of the trading companies, and the remainder to my particular friends, from all of whom I received warm thanks; but from the city I was honoured with substantial notice, viz., an invitation to dine at Guildhall annually on Lord Mayor's day.

The bear-skins I sent to the Empress of Russia, to clothe her majesty and her court in the winter, for which she wrote me a letter of thanks with her own hand and sent it by an ambassador extraordinary, inviting me to share the honours of her bed and crown; but as I never was ambitious of royal dignity, I declined her majesty's favour in the politest terms. The same ambassador had orders to wait and bring my answer to her majesty *personally*, upon which business he was absent about three months: her majesty's reply convinced me of the strength of her affections, and the dignity of her mind; her late indisposition was entirely owing (as she, kind creature! was pleased to express herself in a late conversation with the Prince Dolgoroucki) to my cruelty. What the sex see in me I cannot conceive, but the Empress is not the only female sovereign who has offered me her hand.

Some people have very illiberally reported that Captain Phipps did not proceed as far as he might have done upon that expedition. Here it becomes my duty to acquit him; our ship was in a very proper trim till I loaded it with such an immense quantity of bear-skins and ham, after which it would have been madness to have attempted to proceed further, as we were now scarcely able to combat a brisk gale, much less those mountains of ice which lay in the higher latitudes.

The captain has since often expressed a dissatisfaction that he had no share in the honours of that day, which he emphatically called *bear-skin day*. He has also been very desirous of knowing by what art I destroyed so many thousands, without fatigue or danger to myself; indeed, he is so ambitious of dividing the glory with me, that we have actually quarrelled about it, and we are not now upon speaking terms. He boldly asserts I had no merit in deceiving the bears, because I was covered with one of their skins; nay, he declares there is not, in his opinion, in Europe, so complete a bear naturally as himself among the human species.

He is now a noble peer, and I am too well acquainted with good manners to dispute so delicate a point with his lordship.

CHAPTER XIV

Our Baron excels Baron Tott beyond all comparison, yet fails in part of his attempt—Gets into disgrace with the Grand Seignior, who orders his head to be cut off —Escapes, and gets on board a vessel, in which he is carried to Venice—Baron Tott's origin, with some account of that great man's parents—Pope Ganganelli's amour—His Holiness fond of shell-fish.

BARON DE TOTT, IN HIS MEMOIRS, MAKES AS great a parade of a single act as many travellers whose whole lives have been spent in seeing the different parts of the globe; for my part, if I had been blown from Europe to Asia from the mouth of a cannon, I should have boasted less of it afterwards then he has done of only firing off a Turkish piece of ordnance. What he says of this wonderful gun, as near as my memory will serve me, is this:—"The Turks had placed below the castle, and near the city, on the banks of Simois, a celebrated river, an enormous piece of ordnance cast in brass, which would carry a marble ball of eleven hundred pounds weight. I was inclined," says Tott, "to fire it, but I was willing first to judge of its effect; the crowd about me trembled at this proposal, as they asserted it would overthrow not only the castle, but the city also; at length their fears in part subsided, and I was permitted to discharge it. It required not less than three hundred and thirty pounds weight of powder, and the ball weighed, as before mentioned, eleven hundredweight. When the engineer brought the priming, the crowds who were about me retreated back as fast as they could; nay, it was with the utmost difficulty I persuaded the Pacha, who came on purpose, there was no danger: even the engineer who was to discharge it by my direction was considerably alarmed. I took my stand on some stone-work behind the cannon, gave the signal, and felt a shock like that of an earthquake! At the distance of three hundred fathom the ball burst into three pieces; the fragments crossed the strait, rebounded on the opposite mountain, and left the surface of the water all in a foam through the whole breadth of the channel."

This, gentlemen, is, as near as I can recollect, Baron Tott's account of the largest cannon in the known world. Now, when I was there not long since, the anecdote of Tott's firing this tremendous piece was mentioned as a proof of that gentleman's extraordinary courage.

I was determined not to be outdone by a Frenchman, therefore took this very piece upon my shoulder, and, after balancing it properly, jumped into the sea with it, and swam to the opposite shore, from whence I unfortunately attempted to throw it back into its former place. I say unfortunately, for it slipped a little in my hand just as I was about to discharge it, and in consequence of that it fell into the middle of the channel, where it now lies, without a prospect of ever recovering it: and notwithstanding the high favour I was in with the Grand Seignior, as before mentioned, this cruel Turk, as soon as he heard of the loss of his famous piece of ordnance, issued an order to cut off my head. I was immediately informed of it by one of the Sultanas, with whom I was become a great favourite, and she secreted me in her apartment while the officer charged with my execution was, with his assistants, in search of me.

That very night I made my escape on board a vessel bound to Venice, which was then weighing anchor to proceed on her voyage.

The last story, gentlemen, I am not fond of mentioning, as I miscarried in the attempt, and was very near losing my life into the bargain: however, as it contains no impeachment of my honour, I would not withhold it from you.

Now, gentlemen, you all know me, and can have no doubt of my veracity. I will entertain you with the origin of this same swaggering, bouncing Tott.

His reputed father was a native of Berne, in Switzerland; his profession was that of a surveyor of the streets, lanes, and alleys, vulgarly called a scavenger. His mother was a native of the mountains of Savoy, and had a most beautiful large wen on her neck, common to both sexes in that part of the world; she left her parents when young, and sought her fortune in the same city which gave his father birth; she maintained herself while single by acts of kindness to our sex, for she never was known to refuse them any favour they asked, provided they did but pay her some compliment beforehand. This lovely couple met by accident in the street, in consequence of their being both intoxicated, for by reeling to one centre they threw each other down; this created mutual abuse, in which they were complete adepts; they were both carried to the watch-house, and afterwards to the house of correction;

they soon saw the folly of quarrelling, made it up, became fond of each other, and married; but madam returning to her old tricks, his father, who had high notions of honour, soon separated himself from her; she then joined a

family who strolled about with a puppet-show. In time she arrived at Rome where she kept an oyster-stand. You have all heard, no doubt, of Pope Ganganelli, commonly called Clement XIV.: he was remarkably fond of oysters. One Good Friday, as he was passing through this famous city in state, to assist at high mass at St. Peter's Church, he saw this woman's oysters (which were remarkably fine and fresh); he could not proceed without tasting them.

There were about five thousand people in his train; he
ordered them all to stop, and sent word to the church he
could not attend mass till next day; then alighting from
his horse (for the Pope always rides on horseback upon
these occasions) he went into her stall, and ate every oys-
ter she had there, and afterwards retired into the cellar
where she had a few more. This subterraneous apartment
was her kitchen, parlour, and bedchamber. He liked his
situation so much that he discharged all his attendants,
and to make short of the story, His Holiness passed the
whole night there! Before they parted he gave her abso-
lution, not only for every sin she had, but all she might
hereafter commit.

*Now, gentlemen, I have his mother's word for it (and
her honour cannot be doubted), that Baron Tott is the fruit
of that amour. When Tott was born, his mother applied
to His Holiness, as the father of her child; he immediately
placed him under proper people, and as he grew up gave
him a gentleman's education, had him taught the use of
arms, procured him promotion in France, and a title, and
when he died he left him a good estate.*

CHAPTER XV

A further account of the journey from Harwich to Helvoet-
sluys—Description of a number of marine objects never
mentioned by any traveller before—Rocks seen in this passage
equal to the Alps in magnitude; lobsters, crabs, &c., of an ex-
traordinary magnitude—A woman's life saved—The cause of
her falling into the sea—Dr. Hawes' directions followed with
success.

I OMITTED SEVERAL VERY MATERIAL PARTS IN
my father's journey across the English Channel to Holland, which, that they may not be totally lost, I will now
faithfully give you in his own words, as I heard him relate
them to his friends several times.

"On my arrival," says my father, "at Helvoetsluys, I
was observed to breathe with some difficulty; upon the
inhabitants inquiring into the cause, I informed them
that the animal upon whose back I rode from Harwich
across to their shore did not swim! Such is their peculiar form and disposition, that they cannot float or move
upon the surface of the water; he ran with incredible
swiftness upon the sands from shore to shore, driving
fish in millions before him, many of which were quite
different from any I had yet seen, carrying their heads at

the extremity of their tails. I crossed," continued he, "one prodigious range of rocks, equal in height to the Alps (the tops or highest parts of these marine mountains are said to be upwards of one hundred fathoms below the surface of the sea, on the sides of which there was a great variety of tall, noble trees, loaded with marine fruit, such as lobsters, crabs, oysters, scollops, mussels, cockles, &c. &c.; some of which were a cart-load singly! and none less than a porter's! All those which are brought on shore and sold in our markets are of an inferior dwarf kind, or, properly, waterfalls, *i.e.*, fruit shook off the branches of the tree it grows upon by the motion of the water, as those in our gardens are by that of the wind! The lobster-trees appeared the richest, but the crab and oysters were the tallest. The periwinkle is a kind of shrub; it grows at the foot of the oyster-tree, and twines round it as the ivy does the oak. I observed the effect of several accidents by shipwreck, &c., particularly a ship that had been wrecked by striking against a mountain or rock, the top of which lay within three fathoms of the surface. As she sank she fell upon her side, and forced a very large lobster-tree out of its place. It was in the spring, when the lobsters were very young, and many of them being separated by the violence of the shock, they fell upon a crab-tree which was growing below them; they have, like the farina of plants, united, and produced a fish resembling both. I endeavoured to bring one with me, but it was too cumbersome, and my salt-water Pegasus seemed much displeased at every attempt to stop his career whilst I continued upon his back; besides, I was then, though galloping over a mountain of rocks that lay about midway the passage, at least five hundred fathom below the surface of the sea,

and began to find the want of air inconvenient, therefore I had no inclination to prolong the time. Add to this, my situation was in other respects very unpleasant; I met many large fish, who were, if I could judge by their open mouths, not only able, but really wished to devour us; now, as my Rosinante was blind, I had these hungry gentlemen's attempts to guard against, in addition to my other difficulties.

"As we drew near the Dutch shore, and the body of water over our heads did not exceed twenty fathoms, I thought I saw a human figure in a female dress then lying on the sand before me with some signs of life; when I came close I perceived her hand move: I took it into mine, and brought her on shore as a corpse. An apothecary, who had just been instructed by Dr. Hawes (the Baron's father must have lived very lately if Dr. Hawes was his preceptor), of London, treated her properly, and she recovered. She was the rib of a man who commanded a vessel belonging to Helvoetsluys. He was just going out of port on a voyage, when she, hearing he had got a mistress with him, followed him in an open boat. As soon as she had got on the quarter-deck she flew at her husband, and attempted to strike him with such impetuosity, that he thought it most prudent to slip on one side, and let her make the impression of her fingers upon the waves rather than his face: he was not much out in his ideas of the consequence; for meeting no opposition, she went directly overboard, and it was my unfortunate lot to lay the foundation for bringing this happy pair together again.

"I can easily conceive what execrations the husband loaded me with when, on his return, he found this gentle creature waiting his arrival, and learned the means by which she came into the world again. However, great as the injury is which I have done this poor devil, I hope he will die in charity with me, as my motive was good, though the consequences to him are, it must be confessed, horrible."

CHAPTER XVI

This is a very short chapter, but contains a fact for which the Baron's memory ought to be dear to every Englishman, especially those who may hereafter have the misfortune of being made prisoners of war.

ON MY RETURN FROM GIBRALTAR I TRAVELLED by way of France to England. Being a foreigner, this was not attended with any inconvenience to me. I found, in the harbour of Calais, a ship just arrived with a number of English sailors as prisoners of war. I immediately conceived an idea of giving these brave fellows their liberty, which I accomplished as follows:—After forming a pair of large wings, each of them forty yards long, and fourteen wide, and annexing there to myself, I mounted at break of day, when every creature, even the watch upon deck, was fast asleep. As I hovered over the ship I fastened three grappling irons to the tops of the three masts with my sling, and fairly lifted her several yards out of the water, and then proceeded across to Dover, where I arrived in half an hour! Having no further occasion for these wings, I made them a present to the governor of Dover Castle, where they are now exhibited to the curious.

As to the prisoners, and the Frenchmen who guarded

them, they did not awake till they had been near two hours on Dover Pier. The moment the English understood their situation they changed places with their guard, and took back what they had been plundered of, but no more, for they were too generous to retaliate and plunder them in return.

CHAPTER XVII

Voyage eastward—The Baron introduces a friend who never deceived him: wins a hundred guineas by pinning his faith upon that friend's nose—Game started at sea—Some other circumstances which will, it is hoped, afford the reader no small degree of amusement.

IN A VOYAGE WHICH I MADE TO THE EAST Indies with Captain Hamilton, I took a favourite pointer with me; he was, to use a common phrase, worth his weight in gold, for he never deceived me. One day when we were, by the best observations we could make, at least three hundred leagues from land, my dog pointed; I observed him for near an hour with astonishment, and mentioned the circumstance to the captain and every officer on board, asserting that we must be near land, for my dog smelt game. This occasioned a general laugh; but that did not alter in the least the good opinion I had of my dog. After much conversation pro and con, I boldly told the captain I placed more confidence in Tray's nose than I did in the eyes of every seaman on board, and therefore proposed laying the sum I had agreed to pay for my passage (viz., one hundred guineas) that we should find

game within half an hour. The captain (a good, hearty
fellow) laughed again, desired Mr. Crowford the surgeon, who was prepared, to feel my pulse; he did so, and

reported me in perfect health. The following dialogue
between them took place; I overheard it, though spoken
low, and at some distance.

Captain.—His brain is turned; I cannot with honour
accept his wager.

Surgeon.—I am of a different opinion; he is quite sane,
and depends more upon the scent of his dog than he will
upon the judgment of all the officers on board; he will
certainly lose, and he richly merits it.

Captain.—Such a wager cannot be fair on my side;
however, I'll take him up, if I return his money afterwards.

During the above conversation Tray continued in
the same situation, and confirmed me still more in my

former opinion. I proposed the wager a second time, it was then accepted.

Done! and done! were scarcely said on both sides, when some sailors who were fishing in the long-boat, which was made fast to the stern of the ship, harpooned an exceeding large shark, which they brought on board and began to cut up for the purpose of barrelling the oil, when, behold, they found no less than *six brace of live partridges* in this animal's stomach!

They had been so long in that situation, that one of the hens was sitting upon four eggs, and a fifth was hatching when the shark was opened!!! This young bird we brought up by placing it with a litter of kittens that came into the world a few minutes before! The old cat was as fond of it as of any of her own four-legged progeny, and made herself very unhappy, when it flew out of her reach, till it returned again. As to the other partridges, there were four hens amongst them; one or more were, during the voyage, constantly sitting, and consequently we had plenty of game at the captain's table; and in gratitude to poor Tray (for being a means of winning one hundred guineas) I ordered him the bones daily, and sometimes a whole bird.

CHAPTER XVIII

A SECOND TRIP TO THE MOON.

A second visit (but an accidental one) to the moon—The ship driven by a whirlwind a thousand leagues above the surface of the water, where a new atmosphere meets them and carries them into a capacious harbour in the moon—A description of the inhabitants, and their manner of coming into the lunarian world—Animals, customs, weapons, of war, wine, vegetables, &c.

I HAVE ALREADY INFORMED YOU OF ONE TRIP I made to the moon, in search of my silver hatchet; I afterwards made another in a much pleasanter manner, and stayed in it long enough to take notice of several things, which I will endeavour to describe as accurately as my memory will permit.

I went on a voyage of discovery at the request of a distant relation, who had a strange notion that there were people to be found equal in magnitude to those described by Gulliver in the empire of BROBDIGNAG. For my part I always treated that account as fabulous: however, to oblige him, for he had made me his heir, I

undertook it, and sailed for the South seas, where we arrived without meeting with anything remarkable, except
some flying men and women who were playing at leap-
frog, and dancing minuets in the air.

On the eighteenth day after we had passed the Island
of Otaheite, mentioned by Captain Cook as the place
from whence they brought Omai, a hurricane blew our
ship at least one thousand leagues above the surface of
the water, and kept it at that height till a fresh gale arising
filled the sails in every part, and onwards we travelled at
a prodigious rate; thus we proceeded above the clouds
for six weeks. At last we discovered a great land in the
sky, like a shining island, round and bright, where, coming into a convenient harbour, we went on shore, and
soon found it was inhabited. Below us we saw another
earth, containing cities, trees, mountains, rivers, seas,
&c., which we conjectured was this world which we had
left. Here we saw huge figures riding upon vultures of a
prodigious size, and each of them having three heads. To
form some idea of the magnitude of these birds, I must
inform you that each of their wings is as wide and six
times the length of the main sheet of our vessel, which
was about six hundred tons burthen. Thus, instead of riding upon horses, as we do in this world, the inhabitants
of the moon (for we now found we were in Madam Luna)
fly about on these birds. The king, we found, was engaged
in a war with the sun, and he offered me a commission,
but I declined the honour his majesty intended me. Everything in *this* world is of extraordinary magnitude! a
common flea being much larger than one of our sheep: in
making war, their principal weapons are radishes, which
are used as darts: those who are wounded by them die

immediately. Their shields are made of mushrooms, and
their darts (when radishes are out of season) of the tops
of asparagus. Some of the natives of the dog-star are to
be seen here; commerce tempts them to ramble; their
faces are like large mastiffs', with their eyes near the lower
end or tip of their noses: they have no eyelids, but cover
their eyes with the end of their tongues when they go to
sleep; they are generally twenty feet high. As to the natives of the moon, none of them are less in stature than
thirty-six feet: they are not called the human species, but
the cooking animals, for they all dress their food by fire,
as we do, but lose no time at their meals, as they open
their left side, and place the whole quantity at once in
their stomach, then shut it again till the same day in the
next month; for they never indulge themselves with food
more than twelve times a year, or once a month. All but
gluttons and epicures must prefer this method to ours.

There is but one sex either of the cooking or any other
animals in the moon; they are all produced from trees of
various sizes and foliage; that which produces the cooking animal, or human species, is much more beautiful

than any of the others; it has large straight boughs and flesh-coloured leaves, and the fruit it produces are nuts or pods, with hard shells at least two yards long; when they become ripe, which is known from their changing colour, they are gathered with great care, and laid by as long as they think proper: when they choose to animate the seed of these nuts, they throw them into a large cauldron of boiling water, which opens the shells in a few hours, and out jumps the creature.

Nature forms their minds for different pursuits before they come into the world; from one shell comes forth a warrior, from another a philosopher, from a third a divine, from a fourth a lawyer, from a fifth a farmer, from a sixth a clown, &c. &c., and each of them immediately begins to perfect themselves, by practising what they before knew only in theory.

When they grow old they do not die, but turn into air, and dissolve like smoke! As for their drink, they need none; the only evacuations they have are insensible, and by their breath. They have but one finger upon each hand, with which they perform everything in as perfect a manner as we do who have four besides the thumb. Their heads are placed under their right arm, and when they are going to travel, or about any violent exercise, they generally leave them at home, for they can consult them at any distance; this is a very common practice; and when those of rank or quality among the Lunarians have an inclination to see what's going forward among the common people, they stay at home, *i.e.*, the body stays at home, and sends the head only, which is suffered to be present *incog.*, and return at pleasure with an account of what has passed.

The stones of their grapes are exactly like hail; and I am perfectly satisfied that when a storm or high wind in the moon shakes their vines, and breaks the grapes from the stalks, the stones fall down and form our hail showers. I would advise those who are of my opinion to save a quantity of these stones when it hails next, and make Lunarian wine. It is common beverage at St. Luke's. Some material circumstances I had nearly omitted. They put their bellies to the same use as we do a sack, and throw whatever they have occasion for into it, for they can shut and open it again when they please, as they do their stomachs; they are not troubled with bowels, liver, heart, or any other intestines, neither are they encumbered with clothes, nor is there any part of their bodies unseemly or indecent to exhibit.

Their eyes they can take in and out of their places when they please, and can see as well with them in their hand, as in their head! and if by any accident they lose or damage one, they can borrow or purchase another, and see as clearly with it as their own. Dealers in eyes are on that account very numerous in most parts of the moon, and in this article alone all the inhabitants are whimsical: sometimes green and sometimes yellow eyes are the fashion. I know these things appear strange; but if the shadow of a doubt can remain on any person's mind, I say, let him take a voyage there himself, and then he will know I am a traveller of veracity.

CHAPTER XIX

The Baron crosses the Thames without the assistance of a bridge, ship, boat, balloon, or even his own will: rouses himself after a long nap, and destroys a monster who lived upon the destruction of others.

MY FIRST VISIT TO ENGLAND WAS ABOUT THE beginning of the present king's reign. I had occasion to go down to Wapping, to see some goods shipped, which I was sending to some friends at Hamburgh; after that business was over, I took the Tower Wharf in my way back. Here I found the sun very powerful, and I was so much fatigued that I stepped into one of the cannon to compose me, where I fell fast asleep. This was about noon: it was the fourth of June; exactly at one o'clock these cannon were all discharged in memory of the day. They had been all charged that morning, and having no suspicion of my situation, I was shot over the houses on the opposite side of the river, into a farmer's yard, between Bermondsey and Deptford, where I fell upon a large hay-stack, without waking, and continued there in a sound sleep till hay became so extravagantly dear (which was about three months after), that the farmer found it his interest to send his whole stock to market: the stack I

was reposing upon was the largest in the yard, containing above five hundred load; they began to cut that first. I woke with the voices of the people who had ascended the ladders to begin at the top, and got up, totally ignorant of my situation: in attempting to run away I fell upon the farmer to whom the hay belonged, and broke his neck, yet received no injury myself. l afterwards found, to my great consolation, that this fellow was a most detestable character always keeping the produce of his grounds for extravagant markets.

CHAPTER XX

The Baron slips through the world: after paying a visit to Mount Etna he finds himself in the South Sea; visits Vulcan in his passage; gets on board a Dutchman; arrives at an island of cheese, surrounded by a sea of milk; describes some very extraordinary objects —Lose their compass; their ship slips between the teeth of a fish unknown in this part of the world; their difficulty in escaping frown thence, arrive in the Caspian Sea—Starves a bear to death—A few waistcoat anecdotes—In this chapter, which is the longest, the Baron moralizes upon the virtue of veracity.

MR. DRYBONES' "TRAVELS TO SICILY," WHICH I had read with great pleasure, induced me to pay a visit to Mount Etna; my voyage to this place was not attended with any circumstances worth relating. One morning early, three or four days after my arrival, I set out from a cottage where I had slept, within six miles of the foot of the mountain, determined to explore the internal parts, if I perished in the attempt. After three hours' hard labour I found myself at the top; it was then, and had been for upwards of three weeks, raging: its appearance in this state has been so frequently noticed by different travellers, that I will not tire you with descriptions of objects you are already acquainted with. I walked round the edge of the crater, which appeared to be fifty times at least as capacious as the Devil's Punch-Bowl near Petersfield, on the Portsmouth Road, but not so broad at the bottom, as in that part it resembles the contracted part of a funnel more than a punch-bowl. At last, having made up my mind, in I sprang feet foremost; I soon found myself in a warm berth, and my body bruised and burnt in various parts by the red-hot cinders, which, by their violent ascent, opposed my descent: however, my weight soon brought me to the bottom, where I found myself in the midst of noise and clamour, mixed with the most horrid imprecations; after recovering my senses, and feeling a reduction of my pain, I began to look about me. Guess, gentlemen, my astonishment, when I found myself in the company of Vulcan and his Cyclops, who had been quarrelling, for the three weeks before mentioned, about the observation of good order and due subordination, and which had occasioned such alarms for that space of time in the world above. However, my arrival restored peace to the whole society, and Vulcan himself did me the honour of applying plasters to my wounds, which healed them immediately; he also placed refreshments before me, particularly nectar, and other rich wines, such as the gods and goddesses only aspire to. After this repast was over Vulcan ordered Venus to show me every indulgence which my situation required. To describe the apartment, and the couch on which I reposed, is totally impossible, therefore I will not attempt it; let it suffice to say, it exceeds the power of language to do it justice, or speak of that kind-hearted goddess in any terms equal to her merit.

Vulcan gave me a very concise account of Mount

Etna: he said it was nothing more than an accumulation of ashes thrown from his forge; that he was frequently obliged to chastise his people, at whom, in his passion he made it a practice to throw red-hot coals at home, which they often parried with great dexterity, and then threw them up into the world to place them out of his reach, for they never attempted to assault him in return by throwing them back again. "Our quarrels," added he, "last sometimes three or four months, and these appearances of coals or cinders in the world are what I find you mortals call eruptions." Mount Vesuvius, he assured me, was another of his shops, to which he had a passage three hundred and fifty leagues under the bed of the sea, where similar quarrels produced similar eruptions. I should have continued here as an humble attendant upon Madam Venus, but some busy tattlers, who delight in mischief, whispered a tale in Vulcan's ear, which roused in him a fit of jealousy not to be appeased. Without the least previous notice he took me one morning under his arm, as I was waiting upon Venus, agreeable to custom, and carried me to an apartment I had never before seen, in which there was, to all appearance, a *well* with a wide mouth: over this he held me at arm's length, and saying, *"Ungrateful mortal, return to the world from whence you came,"* without giving me the least opportunity of reply, dropped me in the centre. I found myself descending with an increasing rapidity, till the horror of my mind deprived me of all reflection. I suppose I fell into a trance, from which I was suddenly roused by plunging into a large body of water illuminated by the rays of the sun!!

I could, from my infancy, swim well, and play tricks in the water. I now found myself in paradise, considering the horrors of mind I had just been released from. After looking about me some time, I could discover nothing but an expanse of sea, extending beyond the eye in every direction; I also found it very cold, a different climate from Master Vulcan's shop. At last I observed at some distance a body of amazing magnitude, like a huge rock, approaching me; I soon discovered it to be a piece of floating ice; I swam round it till I found a place where I could ascend to the top, which I did, but not without some difficulty. Still I was out of sight of land, and despair returned with double force; however, before night came on I saw a sail, which we approached very fast; when it was within a very small distance I hailed them in German; they answered in Dutch. I then flung myself into the sea, and they threw out a rope, by which I was taken on board. I now inquired where we were, and was informed, in the great Southern Ocean; this opened a discovery which removed all my doubts and difficulties. It was now evident that I had passed from Mount Etna through the centre of the earth to the South Seas: this, gentlemen, was a much shorter cut than going round the world, and which no man has accomplished, or ever attempted, but myself: however, the next time I perform it I will be much more particular in my observations.

I took some refreshment, and went to rest. The Dutch are a very rude sort of people; I related the Etna passage to the officers, exactly as I have done to you, and some of them, particularly the Captain, seemed by his grimace and half-sentence to doubt my veracity; however, as he had kindly taken me on board his vessel, and was then in the very act of administering to my necessities, I pocketed the affront.

I now in my turn began to inquire where they were bound? To which they answered, they were in search of new discoveries; "*and if,*" said they, "*your story is true, a new passage is really discovered, and we shall not return disappointed.*" We were now exactly in Captain Cook's first track, and arrived the next morning in Botany Bay. This place I would by no means recommend to the English government as a receptacle for felons, or place of punishment; it should rather be the reward of merit, nature having most bountifully bestowed her best gifts upon it.

We stayed here but three days; the fourth after our departure a most dreadful storm arose, which in a few hours destroyed all our sails, splintered our bowsprit, and brought down our topmast; it fell directly upon the box that enclosed our compass, which, with the compass, was broken to pieces. Every one who has been at sea knows the consequences of such a misfortune: we now were at a loss where to steer. At length the storm abated, which was followed by a steady, brisk gale, that carried us at least forty knots an hour for six months! [we should suppose the Baron has made a little mistake, and substituted *months* for *days*] when we began to observe an amazing change in everything about us: our spirits became light, our noses were regaled with the most aromatic effluvia imaginable: the sea had also changed its complexion, and from green became white!! Soon after these wonderful alterations we saw land, and not at any great distance an inlet, which we sailed up near sixty leagues; and found it wide and deep, flowing with milk of the most delicious taste. Here we landed, and soon found it was an island consisting of one large cheese: we

discovered this by one of the company fainting away as
soon as we landed: this man always had an aversion to
cheese; when he recovered, he desired the cheese to be
taken from under his feet: upon examination we found
him perfectly right, for the whole island, as before observed, was nothing but a cheese of immense magnitude!
Upon this the inhabitants, who are amazingly numerous,
principally sustain themselves, and it grows every night
in proportion as it is consumed in the day. Here seemed
to be plenty of vines, with bunches of large grapes, which,
upon being pressed, yielded nothing but milk. We saw
the inhabitants running races upon the surface of the
milk: they were upright, comely figures, nine feet high,
have three legs, and but one arm; upon the whole, their
form was graceful, and when they quarrel, they exercise
a straight horn, which grows in adults from the centre of
their foreheads, with great adroitness; they did not sink
at all, but ran and walked upon the surface of the milk, as
we do upon a bowling-green.

Upon this island of cheese grows great plenty of corn,
the ears of which produce loaves of bread, ready made,
of a round form like mushrooms. We discovered, in our
rambles over this cheese, seventeen other rivers of milk,
and ten of wine.

After thirty-eight days' journey we arrived on the opposite side to that on which we landed: here we found
some blue mould, as cheese-eaters call it, from whence
spring all kinds of rich fruit; instead of breeding mites
it produced peaches, nectarines, apricots, and a thousand delicious fruits which we are not acquainted with.
In these trees, which are of an amazing size, were plenty
of birds' nests; amongst others was a kingfisher's of

prodigious magnitude; it was at least twice the circumference of the dome of St. Paul's Church in London. Upon
inspection, this nest was made of huge trees curiously
joined together; there were, let me see (*for I make it a
rule always to speak within compass*), there were upwards
of five hundred eggs in this nest, and each of them was
as large as four common hogsheads, or eight barrels, and
we could not only see, but hear the young ones chirping
within. Having, with great fatigue, cut open one of these
eggs, we let out a young one unfeathered, considerably
larger than twenty full-grown vultures. Just as we had
given this youngster his liberty the old kingfisher lighted,
and seizing our captain, who had been active in breaking
the egg, in one of her claws, flew with him above a mile
high, and then let him drop into the sea, but not till she
had beaten all his teeth out of his mouth with her wings.

Dutchmen generally swim well: he soon joined us,
and we retreated to our ship. On our return we took a
different route, and observed many strange objects. We
shot two wild oxen, each with one horn, also like the inhabitants, except that it sprouted from between the eyes
of these animals; we were afterwards concerned at having destroyed them, as we found, by inquiry, they tamed
these creatures, and used them as we do horses, to ride
upon and draw their carriages; their flesh, we were informed, is excellent, but useless where people live upon
cheese and milk. When we had reached within two days'
journey of the ship we observed three men hanging to a
tall tree by their heels; upon inquiring the cause of their
punishment, I found they had all been travellers, and
upon their return home had deceived their friends by
describing places they never saw, and relating things that

never happened: this gave me no concern, *as I have ever confined myself to facts.*

As soon as we arrived at the ship we unmoored, and set sail from this extraordinary country, when, to our astonishment, all the trees upon shore, of which there were a great number very tall and large, paid their respects to us twice, bowing to exact time, and immediately recovered their former posture, which was quite erect.

By what we could learn of this CHEESE, it was considerably larger than the continent of all Europe!

After sailing three months we knew not where, being still without compass, we arrived in a sea which appeared to be almost black: upon tasting it we found it most excellent wine, and had great difficulty to keep the sailors from getting drunk with it: however, in a few hours we found ourselves surrounded by whales and other animals of an immense magnitude, one of which appeared to be too large for the eye to form a judgment of: we did not see him till we were close to him. This monster drew our ship, with all her masts standing, and sails bent, by suction into his mouth, between his teeth, which were much larger and taller than the mast of a first-rate man-of-war. After we had been in his mouth some time he opened it pretty wide, took in an immense quantity of water, and floated our vessel, which was at least 500 tons burthen, into his stomach; here we lay as quiet as at anchor in a dead calm. The air, to be sure, was rather warm, and very offensive. We found anchors, cables, boats, and barges in abundance, and a considerable number of ships, some laden and some not, which this creature had swallowed. Everything was transacted by torch-light; no sun, no moon, no planet, to make observations from.

We were all generally afloat and aground twice a-day; whenever he drank, it became high water with us; and when he evacuated, we found ourselves aground; upon a moderate computation, he took in more water at a single draught than is generally to be found in the Lake of Geneva, though that is above thirty miles in circumference. On the second day of our confinement in these regions of darkness, I ventured at low water, as we called it when the ship was aground, to ramble with the Captain, and a few of the other officers, with lights in our hands; we met with people of all nations, to the amount of upwards of ten thousand; they were going to hold a council how to recover their liberty; some of them having lived in this animal's stomach several years; there were several children here who had never seen the world, their mothers having lain in repeatedly in this warm situation. Just as the chairman was going to inform us of the business upon which we were assembled, this plaguy fish, becoming thirsty, drank in his usual manner; the water poured in with such impetuosity, that we were all obliged to retreat to our respective ships immediately, or run the risk of being drowned; some were obliged to swim for it, and with difficulty saved their lives. In a few hours after we were more fortunate, we met again just after the monster had evacuated. I was chosen chairman, and the first thing I did was to propose splicing two main-masts together, and the next time he opened his mouth to be ready to wedge them in, so as to prevent his shutting it. It was unanimously approved. One hundred stout men were chosen upon this service. We had scarcely got our masts properly prepared when an opportunity offered; the monster opened his mouth, immediately the top of the mast was placed against the roof, and the other end pierced his tongue, which effectually prevented him from shutting his mouth. As soon as everything in his stomach was afloat, we manned a few boats, who rowed themselves and us into the world. The daylight, after, as near as we could judge, three months' confinement in total darkness, cheered our spirits surprisingly. When we had all taken our leave of this capacious animal, we mustered just a fleet of ninety-five ships, of all nations, who had been in this confined situation.

We left the two masts in his mouth, to prevent others being confined in the same horrid gulf of darkness and filth. Our first object was to learn what part of the world we were in; this we were for some time at a loss to ascertain: at last I found, from former observations, that we were in the Caspian Sea! which washes part of the country of the Calmuck Tartars. How we came here it was impossible to conceive, as this sea has no communication with any other. One of the inhabitants of the Cheese Island, whom I had brought with me, accounted for it thus:—that the monster in whose stomach we had been so long confined had carried us here through some subterraneous passage; however, we pushed to shore, and I was the first who landed. Just as I put my foot upon the ground a large bear leaped upon me with his forepaws; I caught one in each hand, and squeezed him till he cried out most lustily; however, in this position I held him till I starved him to death. You may laugh, gentlemen, but this was soon accomplished, as I prevented him licking his paws. From hence I travelled up to St. Petersburg a second time: here an old friend gave me a most excellent pointer, descended from the famous bitch before-mentioned, that littered while she was hunting a hare. I had the misfortune to have him shot soon after by a blundering sportsman, who fired at him instead of a covey of partridges which he had just set. Of this creature's skin I have had this waistcoat made (showing his waistcoat), which always leads me involuntarily to game if I walk in the fields in the proper season, and when I come within shot, *one of the buttons constantly flies off; and lodges upon the spot where the sport is;* and as the birds rise, being always primed and cocked, I never miss them. Here are now but three buttons left. I shall have a new set sewed on against the shooting season commences.

When a covey of partridges is disturbed in this manner, by the button falling amongst them, they always rise from the ground in a direct line before each other. I one day, by forgetting to take my ramrod out of my gun, shot it straight through a leash, as regularly as if the cook had spitted them. I had forgot to put in any shot, and the rod had been made so hot with the powder, that the birds were completely roasted by the time I reached home.

Since my arrival in England I have accomplished what I had very much at heart, viz., providing for the inhabitant of the Cheese Island, whom I had brought with me. My old friend, Sir William Chambers, who is entirely indebted to me for all his ideas of Chinese gardening, by a description of which he has gained such high reputation; I say, gentlemen, in a discourse which I had with this gentleman, he seemed much distressed for a contrivance to light the lamps at the new buildings, Somerset House; the common mode with ladders, he observed, was both dirty and inconvenient. My native of the Cheese Island

popped into my head; he was only nine feet high when I first brought him from his own country, but was now increased to ten and a half: I introduced him to Sir William, and he is appointed to that honourable office. He is also to carry, under a large cloak, a utensil in each coat pocket, instead of those four which Sir William has *very properly* fixed for private purposes in so conspicuous a situation, the great quadrangle.

He has also obtained from Mr. Pitt the situation of messenger to his Majesty's lords of the bed-chamber, whose principal employment will *now* be, divulging the secrets of the Royal household to their *worthy* Patron.

SUPPLEMENT

Extraordinary flight on the back of an eagle, over France to Gibraltar, South and North America, the Polar Regions, and back to England, within six-and-thirty hours.

ABOUT THE BEGINNING OF HIS PRESENT Majesty's reign I had some business with a distant relation who then lived on the Isle of Thanet; it was a family dispute, and not likely to be finished soon. I made it a practice during my residence there, the weather being fine, to walk out every morning. After a few of these excursions I observed an object upon a great eminence about three miles distant: I extended my walk to it, and found the ruins of an ancient temple: I approached it with admiration and astonishment; the traces of grandeur and magnificence which yet remained were evident proofs of its former splendour: here I could not help lamenting the ravages and devastations of time, of which that once noble structure exhibited such a melancholy proof. I walked round it several times, meditating on the fleeting and transitory nature of all terrestrial things; on the eastern end were the remains of a lofty tower, near forty feet high, overgrown with ivy, the top apparently flat; I surveyed it on every side very minutely, thinking

that if I could gain its summit I should enjoy the most delightful prospect of the circumjacent country. Animated with this hope, I resolved, if possible, to gain the summit, which I at length effected by means of the ivy, though not without great difficulty and danger; the top I found covered with this evergreen, except a large chasm in the middle. After I had surveyed with pleasing wonder the beauties of art and nature that conspired to enrich the scene, curiosity prompted me to sound the opening in the middle, in order to ascertain its depth, as I entertained a suspicion that it might probably communicate with some unexplored subterranean cavern in the hill; but having no line I was at a loss how to proceed. After revolving the matter in my thoughts for some time, I resolved to drop a stone down and listen to the echo: having found one that answered my purpose I placed myself over the hole, with one foot on each side, and stooping down to listen, I dropped the stone, which I had no sooner done than I heard a rustling below, and suddenly a monstrous eagle put up its head right opposite my face, and rising up with irresistible force, carried me away seated on its shoulders: I instantly grasped it round the neck, which was large enough to fill my arms, and its wings, when extended, were ten yards from one extremity to the other. As it rose with a regular ascent, my seat was perfectly easy, and I enjoyed the prospect below with inexpressible pleasure. It hovered over Margate for some time, was seen by several people, and many shots were fired at it; one ball hit the heel of my shoe, but did me no injury. It then directed its course to Dover cliff, where it alighted, and I thought of dismounting, but was prevented by a sudden discharge of musketry from a party of marines that were exercising on the beach; the balls flew about my head, and rattled on the feathers of the eagle like hail-stones, yet I could not perceive it had received any injury. It instantly reascended and flew over the sea towards Calais, but so very high that the Channel seemed to be no broader than the Thames at London Bridge. In a quarter of an hour I found myself over a thick wood in France, where the eagle descended very rapidly, which caused me to slip down to the back part of its head; but alighting on a large tree, and raising its head, I recovered my seat as before, but saw no possibility of disengaging myself without the danger of being killed by the fall; so I determined to sit fast, thinking it would carry me to the Alps, or some other high mountain, where I could dismount without any danger. After resting a few minutes it took wing, flew several times round the wood, and screamed loud enough to be heard across the English Channel. In a few minutes one of the same species arose out of the wood, and flew directly towards us; it surveyed me with evident marks of displeasure, and came very near me. After flying several times round, they both directed their course to the south-west. I soon observed that the one I rode upon could not keep pace with the other, but inclined towards the earth, on account of my weight; its companion perceiving this, turned round and placed itself in such a position that the other could rest its head on its rump; in this manner they proceeded till noon, when I saw the rock of Gibraltar very distinctly. The day being clear, notwithstanding my degree of elevation, the earth's surface appeared just like a map, where land, sea, lakes, rivers, mountains, and the like were perfectly distinguishable; and having some knowledge of

geography, I was at no loss to determine what part of the globe I was in.

Whilst I was contemplating this wonderful prospect a dreadful howling suddenly began all around me, and in a moment I was invested by thousands of small black, deformed, frightful looking creatures, who pressed me on all sides in such a manner that I could neither move hand or foot: but I had not been in their possession more than ten minutes when I heard the most delightful music that can possibly be imagined, which was suddenly changed into a noise the most awful and tremendous, to which the report of cannon, or the loudest claps of thunder could bear no more proportion than the gentle zephyrs of the evening to the most dreadful hurricane; but the shortness of its duration prevented all those fatal effects which a prolongation of it would certainly have been attended with.

The music commenced, and I saw a great number of the most beautiful little creatures seize the other party, and throw them with great violence into something like a snuff-box, which they shut down, and one threw it away with incredible velocity; then turning to me, he said they whom he had secured were a party of devils, who had wandered from their proper habitation; and that the vehicle in which they were enclosed would fly with unabating rapidity for ten thousand years, when it would burst of its own accord, and the devils would recover their liberty and faculties, as at the present moment. He had no sooner finished this relation than the music ceased, and they all disappeared, leaving me in a state of mind bordering on the confines of despair.

When I had recomposed myself a little, and looking

before me with inexpressible pleasure, I observed that the eagles were preparing to light on the peak of Teneriffe: they descended on the top of a rock, but seeing no possible means of escape if I dismounted determined me to remain where I was. The eagles sat down seemingly fatigued, when the heat of the sun soon caused them both to fall asleep, nor did I long resist its fascinating power. In the cool of the evening, when the sun had retired below the horizon, I was roused from sleep by the eagle moving under me; and having stretched myself along its back, I sat up, and reassumed my travelling position, when they both took wing, and having placed themselves as before, directed their course to South America. The moon shining bright during the whole night, I had a fine view of all the islands in those seas.

About the break of day we reached the great continent of America, that part called Terra Firma, and descended on the top of a very high mountain. At this time the moon, far distant in the west, and obscured by dark clouds, but just afforded light sufficient for me to discover a kind of shrubbery all around, bearing fruit something like cabbages, which the eagles began to feed on very eagerly. I endeavoured to discover my situation, but fogs and passing clouds involved me in the thickest darkness, and what rendered the scene still more shocking was the tremendous howling of wild beasts some of which appeared to be very near: however, I determined to keep my seat, imagining that the eagle would carry me away if any of them should make a hostile attempt. When daylight began to appear, I thought of examining the fruit which I had seen the eagles eat, and as some was hanging which I could easily come at, I took out my

knife and cut a slice; but how great was my surprise to
see that it had all the appearance of roast beef regularly
mixed, both fat and lean! I tasted it, and found it well
flavoured and delicious, then cut several large slices and
put in my pocket, where I found a crust of bread which I
had brought from Margate; took it out, and found three
musket-balls that had been lodged in it on Dover cliff.
I extracted them, and cutting a few slices more, made a
hearty meal of bread and cold beef fruit. I then cut down
two of the largest that grew near me, and tying them together with one of my garters, hung them over the eagle's
neck for another occasion, filling my pockets at the same
time. While I was settling these affairs I observed a large
fruit like an inflated bladder, which I wished to try an experiment upon: and striking my knife into one of them,
a fine pure liquor like Hollands gin rushed out, which
the eagles observing, eagerly drank up from the ground.
I cut down the bladder as fast as I could, and saved about
half a pint in the bottom of it, which I tasted, and could
not distinguish it from the best mountain wine. I drank
it all, and found myself greatly refreshed. By this time the
eagles began to stagger against the shrubs. I endeavoured
to keep my seat, but was soon thrown to some distance
among the bushes. In attempting to rise I put my hand
upon a large hedgehog, which happened to lie among the
grass upon its back: it instantly closed round my hand,
so that I found it impossible to shake it off. I struck it
several times against the ground without effect; but while
I was thus employed I heard a rustling among the shrubbery, and looking up, I saw a huge animal within three
yards of me; I could make no defence, but held out both
my hands, when it rushed upon me, and seized that on

which the hedgehog was fixed. My hand being soon relieved, I ran to some distance, where I saw the creature suddenly drop down and expire with the hedgehog in its throat. When the danger was past I went to view the eagles, and found them lying on the grass fast asleep, being intoxicated with the liquor they had drank. Indeed, I found myself considerably elevated by it, and seeing everything quiet, I began to search for some more, which I soon found; and having cut down two large bladders, about a gallon each, I tied them together, and hung them over the neck of the other eagle, and the two smaller ones I tied with a cord round my own waist. Having secured a good stock of provisions, and perceiving the eagles begin to recover, I again took my seat. In half an hour they arose majestically from the place, without taking the least notice of their incumbrance. Each reassumed its former station; and directing their course to the northward, they crossed the Gulf of Mexico, entered North America, and steered directly for the Polar regions, which gave me the finest opportunity of viewing this vast continent that can possibly be imagined.

Before we entered the frigid zone the cold began to affect me; but piercing one of my bladders, I took a draught, and found that it could make no impression on me afterwards. Passing over Hudson's Bay, I saw several of the Company's ships lying at anchor, and many tribes of Indians marching with their furs to market.

By this time I was so reconciled to my seat; and become such an expert rider, that I could sit up and look around me; but in general I lay along the eagle's neck, grasping it in my arms, with my hands immersed in its feathers, in order to keep them warm.

In these cold climates I observed that the eagles flew with greater rapidity, in order, I suppose, to keep their blood in circulation. In passing Baffin's Bay I saw several large Greenlandmen to the eastward, and many surprising mountains of ice in those seas.

While I was surveying these wonders of nature it occurred to me that this was a good opportunity to discover the north-west passage, if any such thing existed, and not only obtain the reward offered by government, but the honour of a discovery pregnant with so many advantages to every European nation. But while my thoughts were absorbed in this pleasing reverie I was alarmed by the first eagle striking its head against a solid transparent substance, and in a moment that which I rode experienced the same fate, and both fell down seemingly dead.

Here our lives must inevitably have terminated, had not a sense of danger, and the singularity of my situation, inspired me with a degree of skill and dexterity which enabled us to fall near two miles perpendicular with as little inconveniency as if we had been let down with a rope: for no sooner did I perceive the eagles strike against a frozen cloud, which is very common near the poles, than (they being close together) I laid myself along the back of the foremost, and took hold of its wings to keep them extended, at the same time stretching out my legs behind to support the wings of the other. This had the desired effect, and we descended very safe on a mountain of ice, which I supposed to be about three miles above the level of the sea.

I dismounted, unloaded the eagles, opened one of the bladders, and administered some of the liquor to each of them, without once considering that the horrors of destruction seemed to have conspired against me. The roaring of waves, crashing of ice, and the howling of bears, conspired to form a scene the most awful and tremendous: but notwithstanding this, my concern for the recovery of the eagles was so great, that I was insensible of the danger to which I was exposed. Having rendered them every assistance in my power, I stood over them in painful anxiety, fully sensible that it was only by means of them that I could possibly be delivered from these abodes of despair.

But suddenly a monstrous bear began to roar behind me, with a voice like thunder. I turned round, and seeing the creature just ready to devour me, having the bladder of liquor in my hands, through fear I squeezed it so hard, that it burst, and the liquor flying in the eyes of the animal, totally deprived it of sight. It instantly turned from me, ran away in a state of distraction, and soon fell over a precipice of ice into the sea, where I saw it no more.

The danger being over, I again turned my attention to the eagles, whom I found in a fair way of recovery, and suspecting that they were faint for want of victuals, I took one of the beef fruit, cut it into small slices, and presented them with it, which they devoured with avidity.

Having given them plenty to eat and drink, and disposed of the remainder of my provision, I took possession of my seat as before. After composing myself, and adjusting everything in the best manner, I began to eat and drink very heartily; and through the effects of the mountain wine, as I called it, was very cheerful, and began to sing a few verses of a song which I had learned when I was a boy: but the noise soon alarmed the eagles, who had been asleep, through the quantity of liquor which they had drank, and they arose seemingly much terrified.

Happily for me, however, when I was feeding them I had accidentally turned their heads towards the south-east, which course they pursued with a rapid motion. In a few hours I saw the Western Isles, and soon after had the inexpressible pleasure of seeing Old England. I took no notice of the seas or islands over which I passed.

The eagles descended gradually as they drew near the shore, intending, as I supposed, to alight on one of the Welsh mountains; but when they came to the distance of about sixty yards two guns were fired at them, loaded with balls, one of which took place in a bladder of liquor that hung to my waist; the other entered the breast of the foremost eagle, who fell to the ground, while that which I rode, having received no injury, flew away with amazing swiftness.

This circumstance alarmed me exceedingly, and I began to think it was impossible for me to escape with my life; but recovering a little, I once more looked down upon the earth, when, to my inexpressible joy, I saw Margate at a little distance, and the eagle descending on the old tower whence it had carried me on the morning of the day before. It no sooner came down than I threw myself off, happy to find that I was once more restored to the world. The eagle flew away in a few minutes, and I sat down to compose my fluttering spirits, which I did in a few hours.

I soon paid a visit to my friends, and related these adventures. Amazement stood in every countenance; their congratulations on my returning in safety were repeated with an unaffected degree of pleasure, and we passed the evening as we are doing now, every person present paying the highest compliments to my COURAGE and VERACITY.

PREFACE

BARON MUNCHAUSEN HAS CERTAINLY BEEN productive of much benefit to the literary world; the numbers of egregious travellers have been such, that they demanded a very Gulliver to surpass them. If Baron de Tott dauntlessly discharged an enormous piece of artillery, the Baron Munchausen has done more; he has taken it and swam with it across the sea. When travellers are solicitous to be the heroes of their own story, surely they must admit to superiority, and blush at seeing themselves out-done by the renowned Munchausen: I doubt whether any one hitherto, Pantagruel, Gargantua, Captain Lemuel, or De Tott, has been able to out-do our Baron in this species of excellence: and as at present our curiosity seems much directed to the interior of Africa, it must be edifying to have the real relation of Munchausen's adventures there before any further intelligence arrives; for he seems to adapt himself and his exploits to the spirit of the times, and recounts what he thinks should be most interesting to his auditors.

I do not say that the Baron, in the following stories, means a satire on any political matters whatever. No; but if the reader understands them so, I cannot help it.

If the Baron meets with a parcel of negro ships carrying whites into slavery to work upon their plantations
in a cold climate, should we therefore imagine that he
intends a reflection on the present traffic in human flesh?
And that, if the negroes should do so, it would be simple
justice, as retaliation is the law of God! If we were to think
this a reflection on any present commercial or political
matter, we should be tempted to imagine, perhaps, some
political ideas conveyed in every page, in every sentence
of the whole. Whether such things are or are not the intentions of the Baron the reader must judge.

We have had not only wonderful travellers in this vile
world, but splenetic travellers, and of these not a few, and
also conspicuous enough. It is a pity, therefore, that the
Baron has not endeavoured to surpass them also in this
species of story-telling. Who is it can read the travels of
Smellfungus, as Sterne calls him, without admiration? To
think that a person from the North of Scotland should
travel through some of the finest countries in Europe, and
find fault with everything he meets—nothing to please
him! And therefore, methinks, the Tour to the Hebrides
is more excusable, and also perhaps Mr. Twiss's Tour in
Ireland. Dr. Johnson, bred in the luxuriance of London,
with more reason should become cross and splenetic in
the bleak and dreary regions of the Hebrides.

The Baron, in the following work, seems to be sometimes philosophical; his account of the language of the
interior of Africa, and its analogy with that of the inhabitants of the moon, show him to be profoundly versed in
the etymological antiquities of nations, and throw new
light upon the abstruse history of the ancient Scythians,
and the Collectanea.

His endeavour to abolish the custom of eating live flesh in the interior of Africa, as described in Bruce's Travels, is truly humane. But far be it from me to suppose, that by Gog and Magog and the Lord Mayor's show he means a satire upon any person or body of persons whatever: or, by a tedious litigated trial of blind judges and dumb matrons following a wild goose chase all round the world, he should glance at any trial whatever.

Nevertheless, I must allow that it was extremely presumptuous in Munchausen to tell half the sovereigns of the world that they were wrong, and advise them what they ought to do; and that instead of ordering millions of their subjects to massacre one another, it would be more to their interest to employ their forces in concert for the general good; as if he knew better than the Empress of Russia, the Grand Vizier, Prince Potemkin, or any other butcher in the world. But that he should be a royal Aristocrat, and take the part of the injured Queen of France in the present political drama, I am not at all surprised; but I suppose his mind was fired by reading the pamphlet written by Mr. Burke.

THE SECOND VOLUME

CHAPTER XXI

The Baron insists on the veracity of his former Memoirs—Forms a design of making discoveries in the interior parts of Africa—His discourse with Hilaro Frosticos about it—His conversation with Lady Fragrantia—The Baron goes, with other persons of distinction, to Court; relates an anecdote of the Marquis de Bellecourt.

ALL THAT I HAVE RELATED BEFORE, SAID THE Baron, is gospel; and if there be any one so hardy as to deny it, I am ready to fight him with any weapon he pleases. Yes, cried he, in a more elevated tone, as he started from his seat, I will condemn him to swallow this decanter, glass and all perhaps, and filled with kerren-wasser [a kind of ardent spirit distilled from cherries, and much used in some parts of Germany]. Therefore, my dear friends and companions, have confidence in what I say, and pay honour to the tales of Munchausen. A traveller has a right to relate and embellish his adventures as he pleases, and it is very unpolite to refuse that deference and applause they deserve.

Having passed some time in England since the completion of my former memoirs, I at length began to revolve in my mind what a prodigious field of discovery must be in the interior part of Africa. I could not sleep with the thoughts of it; I therefore determined to gain every proper assistance from Government to penetrate the celebrated source of the Nile and assume the viceroyship of the interior kingdoms of Africa, or, at least, the great realm of Monomotapa. It was happy for me that I had one most powerful friend at court, whom I shall call the illustrious Hilaro Frosticos. You perchance know him not by that name; but we had a language among ourselves, as well we may, for in the course of my peregrinations I have acquired precisely nine hundred and ninety-nine leash of languages. What! gentlemen, do you stare? Well, I allow there are not so many languages spoken in this vile world; but then, have I not been in the moon? and trust me, whenever I write a treatise upon education, I shall delineate methods of inculcating whole dozens of languages at once, French, Spanish, Greek, Hebrew, Cherokee, &c., in such a style as will shame all the pedagogues existing.

Having passed a whole night without being able to sleep for the vivid imagination of African discoveries, I hastened to the levee of my illustrious friend Hilaro Frosticos, and having mentioned my intention with all the vigour of fancy, he gravely considered my words, and after some awful meditations thus he spoke: *Olough, ma genesat, istum fullanah, cum dera kargos belgarasah eseum balgo bartigos triangulissimus!* However, added he, it behoveth thee to consider and ponder well upon the perils and the multitudinous dangers in the way of that wight who thus advanceth in all the perambulation of adventures: and verily, most valiant sire and Baron, I hope thou wilt demean thyself with all that laudable gravity and precaution which, as is related in the three hundred and forty-seventh chapter of the Prophilactics, is of more consideration than all the merit in this terraqueous globe. Yes, most truly do I advise thee unto thy good, and speak unto thee, most valiant Munchausen, with the greatest esteem, and wish thee to succeed in thy voyage; for it is said, that in the interior realms of Africa there are tribes that can see but just three inches and a half beyond the extremity of their noses; and verily thou shouldest moderate thyself, even sure and slow; they stumble who walk fast. But we shall bring you unto the Lady Fragrantia, and have her opinion of the matter. He then took from his pocket a cap of dignity, such as described in the most honourable and antique heraldry, and placing it upon my head, addressed me thus:—"As thou seemest again to revive the spirit of ancient adventure, permit me to place upon thy head this favour, as a mark of the esteem in which I hold thy valorous disposition."

The Lady Fragrantia, my dear friends, was one of the most divine creatures in all Great Britain, and was desperately in love with me. She was drawing my portrait upon a piece of white satin, when the most noble Hilaro Frosticos advanced. He pointed to the cap of dignity which he had placed upon my head. "I do declare, Hilaro," said the lovely Fragrantia, "'tis pretty, 'tis interesting; I love you, and I like you, my dear Baron," said she, putting on another plume: "this gives it an air more delicate and more fantastical. I do thus, my dear Munchausen, as your friend, yet you can reject or accept my present just as you

W.S.

please; but I like the fancy, 'tis a good one, and I mean to improve it: and against whatever enemies you go, I shall have the sweet satisfaction to remember you bear my favour on your head!"

I snatched it with trepidation, and gracefully dropping on my knees, I three times kissed it with all the rapture of romantic love. "I swear," cried I, "by thy bright eyes, and by the lovely whiteness of thine arm, that no savage, tyrant, or enemy upon the face of the earth shall despoil me of this favour, while one drop of the blood of the Munchausens doth circulate in my veins! I will bear it triumphant through the realms of Africa, whither I now intend my course, and make it respected, even in the court of Prester John."

"I admire your spirit," replied she, "and shall use my utmost interest at court to have you dispatched with every pomp, and as soon as possible, but here comes a most brilliant company indeed, Lady Carolina Wilhelmina Amelia Skeggs, Lord Spigot, and Lady Faucet, and the Countess of Belleair."

After the ceremonies of introduction to this company were over, we proceeded to consult upon the business; and as the cause met with general applause, it was immediately determined that I should proceed without delay, as soon as I obtained the sovereign approbation. "I am convinced," said Lord Spigot, "that if there be any thing really unknown and worthy of our most ardent curiosity, it must be in the immense regions of Africa; that country, which seems to be the oldest on the globe, and yet with the greater part of which we are almost utterly unacquainted; what prodigious wealth of gold and diamonds must not lie concealed in those torrid regions, when the very rivers on the coast pour forth continual specimens of golden sand! 'Tis my opinion, therefore, that the Baron deserves the applause of all Europe for his spirit, and merits the most powerful assistance of the sovereign."

So flattering an approbation, you may be sure, was delightful to my heart, and with every confidence and joy I suffered them to take me to court that instant. After the usual ceremonies of introduction, suffice it to say that I met with every honour and applause that my most sanguine expectations could demand. I had always a taste for the fashionable *je ne sais quoi* of the most elegant society, and in the presence of all the sovereigns of Europe I ever found myself quite at home, and experienced from the whole court the most flattering esteem and admiration. I remember, one particular day, the fate of the unfortunate Marquis de Bellecourt. The Countess of Rassinda, who accompanied him, looked most divinely. "Yes, I am confident," said the Marquis de Bellecourt to me, "that I have acted according to the strictest sentiments of justice and of loyalty to my sovereign. What stronger breast-plate than a heart untainted? and though I did not receive a word nor a look, yet I cannot think—no, it were impossible to be misrepresented. Conscious of my own integrity, I will try again—I will go boldly up." The Marquis de Bellecourt saw the opportunity; he advanced three paces, put his hand upon his breast and bowed. "Permit me," said he, "with the most profound respect, to ——" His tongue faltered—he could scarcely believe his sight, for at that moment the whole company were moving out of the room. He found himself almost alone, deserted by every one. "What!" said he, "and did he turn upon his heel with the most marked contempt? Would he not speak to me? Would he not even hear me utter a word in my defence?" His heart died within him—not even a look, a smile from any one. "My friends! Do they not know me? Do they not see me? Alas! they fear to catch the contagion of my ——. Then," said he, "adieu!—'tis more than I can bear. I shall go to my country seat, and never, never will return. Adieu, fond court, adieu!—"

The venerable Marquis de Bellecourt stopped for a moment ere he entered his carriage. Thrice he looked back, and thrice he wiped the starting tear from his eye. "Yes," said he, "for once, at least, truth shall be found—in the bottom of a well!"

Peace to thy ghost, most noble marquis! a King of kings shall pity thee; and thousands who are yet unborn shall owe their happiness to thee, and have cause to bless the thousands, perhaps, that shall never even know thy name; but Munchausen's self shall celebrate thy glory!

CHAPTER XXII

Preparations for the Baron's expedition into Africa—Description of his chariot; the beauties of its interior decorations; the animals that drew it, and the mechanism of the wheels.

EVERYTHING BEING CONCLUDED, AND HAVING received my instructions for the voyage, I was conducted by the illustrious Hilaro Frosticos, the Lady Fragrantia, and a prodigious crowd of nobility and placed sitting upon the summit of the whale's bones at the palace; and having remained in this situation for three days and three nights, as a trial ordeal, and a specimen of my perseverance and resolution, the third hour after midnight they seated me in the chariot of Queen Mab. It was of a prodigious dimension, large enough to contain more stowage than the tun of Heidelberg, and globular like a hazelnut: in fact, it seemed to be really a hazel-nut grown to a most extravagant dimension, and that a great worm of proportionable enormity had bored a hole in the shell. Through this same entrance I was ushered. It was as large as a coach-door, and I took my seat in the centre, a kind of chair self-balanced without touching anything, like the fancied tomb of Mahomet. The whole interior surface of the nutshell appeared a luminous representation of all the stars of heaven, the fixed stars, the planets, and a comet. The stars were as large as those worn by our first nobility, and the comet, excessively brilliant, seemed as if you had assembled all the eyes of the beautiful girls in the kingdom, and combined them, like a peacock's plumage, into the form of a comet—that is, a globe, and a bearded tail to it, diminishing gradually to a point. This beautiful constellation seemed very sportive and delightful. It was much in the form of a tadpole! and, without ceasing, went, full of playful giddiness, up and down, all over the heaven on the concave surface of the nutshell. One time it would be at that part of the heavens under my feet, and in the next minute would be over my head. It was never at rest, but for ever going east, west, north, or south, and paid no more respect to the different worlds than if they were so many lanterns without reflectors. Some of them he would dash against and push out of their places; others he would burn up and consume to ashes: and others again he would split into fritters, and their fragments would instantly take a globular form, like spilled quicksilver, and become satellites to whatever other worlds they should happen to meet with in their career. In short, the whole seemed an epitome of the creation, past, present, and future; and all that passes among the stars during one thousand years was here generally performed in as many seconds.

I surveyed all the beauties of the chariot with wonder and delight. "Certainly," cried I, "this is heaven in miniature!" In short, I took the reins in my hand. But before I proceed on my adventures, I shall mention the rest of my attendant furniture. The chariot was drawn by a team of nine bulls harnessed to it, three after three. In the first rank was a most tremendous bull named John Mowmowsky; the rest were called Jacks in general, but not dignified by any particular denomination. They were all shod for the journey, not indeed like horses, with iron, or as bullocks commonly are, to drag on a cart; but were shod with men's skulls. Each of their feet was, hoof and all, crammed into a man's head, cut off for the purpose, and fastened therein with a kind of cement or paste, so that the skull seemed to be a part of the foot and hoof of the animal. With these skull-shoes the creatures could perform astonishing journeys, and slide upon the water, or upon the ocean, with great velocity. The harnesses were fastened with golden buckles, and decked with studs in a superb style, and the creatures were ridden by nine postillions, crickets of a great size, as large as monkeys, who sat squat upon the heads of the bulls, and were continually chirping at a most infernal rate, loud in proportion to their bodies.

The wheels of the chariot consisted of upwards of ten thousand springs, formed so as to give the greater impetuosity to the vehicle, and were more complex than a dozen clocks like that of Strasburgh. The external of the chariot was adorned with banners, and a superb festoon of laurel that formerly shaded me on horseback. And now, having given you a very concise description of my machine for travelling into Africa, which you must allow to be far superior to the apparatus of Monsieur Vaillant, I shall proceed to relate the exploits of my voyage.

CHAPTER XXIII

The Baron proceeds on his voyage—Convoys a squadron to Gi-braltar—Declines the acceptance of the island of Candia—His chariot damaged by Pompey's Pillar and Cleopatra's needle—The Baron out-does Alexander—Breaks his chariot, and splits a great rock at the Cape of Good Hope.

TAKING THE REINS IN MY HAND, WHILE THE music gave a general salute, I cracked my whip, away they went, and in three hours I found myself just between the Isle of Wight and the main land of England. Here I remained four days, until I had received part of my ac-companiment, which I was ordered to take under my convoy. 'Twas a squadron of men-of-war that had been a long time prepared for the Baltic, but which were now destined for the Mediterranean. By the assistance of large hooks and eyes, exactly such as are worn in our hats, but of a greater size, some hundredweight each, the men-of-war hooked themselves on to the wheels of the vehicle: and, in fact, nothing could be more simple or convenient, because they could be hooked or unhooked in an instant with the utmost facility. In short, having given a general discharge of their artillery, and three cheers, I cracked my whip, away we went, helter skelter, and in six jiffies I found myself and all my retinue safe and in good spirits just at the rock of Gibraltar. Here I unhooked my squadron, and having taken an affectionate leave of the officers, I suffered them to proceed in their ordinary manner to the place of their destination. The whole garrison were highly delighted with the novelty of my vehicle; and at the pressing solicitations of the governor and officers I went ashore, and took a view of that barren old rock, about which more powder has been fired away than would purchase twice as much fertile ground in any part of the world! Mounting my chariot, I took the reins, and again made forward, in mad career, down the Mediterranean to the isle of Candia. Here I received despatches from the Sublime Porte, entreating me to assist in the war against Russia, with a reward of the whole island of Candia for my alliance. At first I hesitated, thinking that the island of Candia would be a most valuable acquisition to the sovereign who at that time employed me, and that the most delicious wines, sugar, &c., in abundance would flourish on the island; yet, when I considered the trade of the East India Company, which would most probably suffer by the intercourse with Persia through the Mediterranean, I at once rejected the proposal, and had afterwards the thanks of the Honourable the House of Commons for my propriety and political discernment.

Having been properly refreshed at Candia, I again proceeded, and in a short time arrived in the land of Egypt. The land of this country, at least that part of it near the sea, is very low, so that I came upon it ere I was aware, and the Pillar of Pompey got entangled in the various wheels of the machine, and damaged the whole considerably. Still I drove on through thick and thin, till, passing

over that great obelisk, the Needle of Cleopatra, the work
got entangled again, and jolted at a miserable rate over
the mud and swampy ground of all that country; yet my
poor bulls trotted on with astonishing labour across the
Isthmus of Suez into the Red Sea, and left a track, an obscure channel, which has since been taken by De Tott for
the remains of a canal cut by some of the Ptolemies from
the Red Sea to the Mediterranean; but, as you perceive,
was in reality no more than the track of my chariot, the
car of Queen Mab.

As the artists at present in that country are nothing
wonderful, though the ancient Egyptians, 'tis said, were
most astonishing fellows, I could not procure any new
coach-springs, or have a possibility of setting my machine to rights in the kingdom of Egypt; and as I could
not presume to attempt another journey overland, and
the great mountains of marble beyond the source of the
Nile, I thought it most eligible to make the best way I
could, by sea, to the Cape of Good Hope, where I supposed I should get some Dutch smiths and carpenters,
or perhaps some English artists; and my vehicle being
properly repaired, it was my intention thence to proceed,
overland, through the heart of Africa. The surface of the
water, I well knew, afforded less resistance to the wheels
of the machine—it passed along the waves like the chariot of Neptune; and in short, having gotten upon the Red
Sea, we scudded away to admiration through the pass of
Babelmandeb to the great Western coast of Africa, where
Alexander had not the courage to venture.

And really, my friends, if Alexander had ventured toward the Cape of Good Hope he most probably would
have never returned. It is difficult to determine whether

there were then any inhabitants in the more southern
parts of Africa or not; yet, at any rate, this conqueror of the
world would have made but a nonsensical adventure; his
miserable ships, not contrived for a long voyage, would
have become leaky, and foundered, before he could have

doubled the Cape, and left his Majesty fairly beyond the
limits of the then known world. Yet it would have been
an august exit for an Alexander, after having subdued
Persia and India, to be wandering the Lord knows where,
to Jup or Ammon, perhaps, or on a voyage to the moon,
as an Indian chief once said to Captain Cook.

But, for my part, I was far more successful than Alexander; I drove on with the most amazing rapidity, and thinking to halt on shore at the Cape, I unfortunately drove too close, and shattered the right side wheels of my vehicle against the rock, now called the Table Mountain. The machine went against it with such impetuosity as completely shivered the rock in a horizontal direction; so that the summit of the mountain, in the form of a semi-sphere, was knocked into the sea, and the steep mountain becoming thereby flattened at the top, has since received the name of the Table Mountain, from its similarity to that piece of furniture.

Just as this part of the mountain was knocked off, the ghost of the Cape, that tremendous sprite which cuts such a figure in the Lusiad, was discovered sitting squat in an excavation formed for him in the centre of the mountain. He seemed just like a young bee in his little cell before he comes forth, or like a bean in a bean-pod; and when the upper part of the mountain was split across and knocked off, the superior half of his person was discovered. He appeared of a bottle-blue colour, and started, dazzled with the unexpected glare of the light hearing the dreadful rattle of the wheels, and the loud chirping of the crickets, he was thunder-struck, and instantly giving a shriek, sunk down ten thousand fathoms into the earth, while the mountain, vomiting out some smoke, silently closed up, and left not a trace behind!

CHAPTER XXIV

The Baron secures his chariot, &c., at the Cape and takes his passage for England in a homeward-bound Indiaman— Wrecked upon an island of ice, near the coast of Guinea —Escapes from the wreck, and rears a variety of vegetables upon the island—Meets some vessels belonging to the negroes bringing white slaves from Europe, in retaliation, to work upon their plantations in a cold climate near the South Pole—Arrives in England, and lays an account of his expedition before the Privy Council—Great preparations for a new expedition—The Sphinx, Gog and Magog, and a great company attend him—The ideas of Hilaro Frosticos respecting the interior parts of Africa.

I PERCEIVED WITH GRIEF AND CONSTERNATION the miscarriage of all my apparatus; yet I was not absolutely dejected: a great mind is never known but in adversity. With permission of the Dutch governor the chariot was properly laid up in a great storehouse, erected at the water's edge, and the bulls received every refreshment possible after so terrible a voyage. Well, you may be sure they deserved it, and therefore every attendance was engaged for them, until I should return.

As it was not possible to do anything more I took my passage in a homeward-bound Indiaman, to return to

London, and lay the matter before the Privy Council.
We met with nothing particular until we arrived upon
the coast of Guinea, where, to our utter astonishment,
we perceived a great hill, seemingly of glass, advancing
against us in the open sea; the rays of the sun were re-
flected upon it with such splendour, that it was extremely
difficult to gaze at the phenomenon. I immediately knew
it to be an island of ice, and though in so very warm a
latitude, determined to make all possible sail from such
horrible danger. We did so, but all in vain, for about
eleven o'clock at night, blowing a very hard gale, and
exceedingly dark, we struck upon the island. Nothing
could equal the distraction, the shrieks, and despair of
the whole crew, until I, knowing there was not a moment
to be lost, cheered up their spirits, and bade them not
despond, but do as I should request them. In a few minutes the vessel was half full of water, and the enormous
castle of ice that seemed to hem us in on every side, in
some places falling in hideous fragments upon the deck,
killed one half of the crew; upon which, getting upon the
summit of the mast, I contrived to make it fast to a great
promontory of the ice, and calling to the remainder of
the crew to follow me, we all escaped from the wreck,
and got upon the summit of the island.

The rising sun soon gave us a dreadful prospect of
our situation, and the loss, or rather iceification, of the
vessel; for being closed in on every side with castles of
ice during the night, she was absolutely frozen over and
buried in such a manner that we could behold her under our feet, even in the central solidity of the island.
Having debated what was best to be done, we immediately cut down through the ice and got up some of the

cables of the vessel, and the boats, which, making fast to
the island, we towed it with all our might, determined
to bring home island and all, or perish in the attempt.
On the summit of the island we placed what oakum and
dregs of every kind of matter we could get from the vessel, which, in the space of a very few hours, on account of
the liquefying of the ice, and the warmth of the sun, were
transformed into a very fine manure; and as I had some
seeds of exotic vegetables in my pocket, we shortly had
a sufficiency of fruits and roots growing upon the island
to supply the whole crew, especially the bread-fruit tree,
a few plants of which had been in the vessel; and another
tree, which bore plum-puddings so very hot, and with
such exquisite proportion of sugar, fruit, &c., that we all
acknowledged it was not possible to taste anything of
the kind more delicious in England: in short, though the
scurvy had made such dreadful progress among the crew
before our striking upon the ice, the supply of vegetables,
and especially the bread-fruit and pudding-fruit, put an
almost immediate stop to the distemper.

We had not proceeded thus many weeks, advancing
with incredible fatigue by continual towing, when we fell
in with a fleet of Negro-men, as they call them. These
wretches, I must inform you, my dear friends, had found
means to make prizes of those vessels from some Europeans upon the coast of Guinea, and tasting the sweets
of luxury, had formed colonies in several new discovered
islands near the south pole, where they had a variety of
plantations of such matters as would only grow in the
coldest climates. As the black inhabitants of Guinea were
unsuited to the climate and excessive cold of the country,
they formed the diabolical project of getting Christian

slaves to work for them. For this purpose they sent vessels every year to the coast of Scotland, the northern parts of Ireland and Wales, and were even sometimes seen off the coast of Cornwall. And having purchased, or entrapped by fraud or violence, a great number of men, women, and children, they proceeded with their cargoes of human flesh to the other end of the world, and sold them to their planters, where they were flogged into obedience, and made to work like horses all the rest of their lives.

My blood ran cold at the idea, while every one on the island also expressed his horror that such an iniquitous traffic should be suffered to exist. But, except by open violence, it was found impossible to destroy the trade, on account of a barbarous prejudice, entertained of late by the negroes, that the white people have no souls! However, we were determined to attack them, and steering down our island upon them, soon overwhelmed them: we saved as many of the white people as possible, but pushed all the blacks into the water again. The poor creatures we saved from slavery were so overjoyed, that they wept aloud through gratitude, and we experienced every delightful sensation to think what happiness we should shower upon their parents, their brothers and sisters and children, by bringing them home safe, redeemed from slavery, to the bosom of their native country.

Having happily arrived in England, I immediately laid a statement of my voyage, &c., before the Privy Council, and entreated an immediate assistance to travel into Africa, and, if possible, refit my former machine, and take it along with the rest. Everything was instantly granted to my satisfaction, and I received orders to get myself ready for departure as soon as possible.

As the Emperor of China had sent a most curious animal as a present to Europe, which was kept in the Tower, and it being of an enormous stature, and capable of performing the voyage with *éclat*, she was ordered to attend me. She was called Sphinx, and was one of the most tremendous though magnificent figures I ever beheld. She was harnessed with superb trappings to a large flat-bottomed boat, in which was placed an edifice of wood, exactly resembling Westminster Hall. Two balloons were placed over it, tackled by a number of ropes to the boat, to keep up a proper equilibrium, and prevent it from overturning, or filling, from the prodigious weight of the fabric.

The interior of the edifice was decorated with seats, in the form of an amphitheatre, and crammed as full as it could hold with ladies and lords, as a council and retinue for your humble servant. Nearly in the centre was a seat elegantly decorated for myself, and on either side of me were placed the famous Gog and Magog in all their pomp.

The Lord Viscount Gosamer being our postillion, we floated gallantly down the river, the noble Sphinx gambolling like the huge leviathan, and towing after her the boat and balloons.

Thus we advanced, sailing gently, into the open sea; being calm weather, we could scarcely feel the motion of the vehicle, and passed our time in grand debate upon the glorious intention of our voyage, and the discoveries that would result.

"I am of opinion," said my noble friend, Hilaro Frosticos, "that Africa was originally inhabited for the greater part, or, I may say, subjugated by lions which, next to man, seem to be the most dreaded of all mortal tyrants. The country in general—at least, what we have been hitherto able to discover, seems rather inimical to human life; the intolerable dryness of the place, the burning sands that overwhelm whole armies and cities in general ruin, and the hideous life many roving hordes are compelled to lead, incline me to think, that if ever we form any great settlements therein, it will become the grave of our countrymen. Yet it is nearer to us than the East Indies, and I cannot but imagine, that in many places every production of China, and of the East and West Indies, would flourish, if properly attended to. And as the country is so prodigiously extensive and unknown, what a source of discovery must not it contain! In fact, we know less about the interior of Africa than we do of the moon; for in this latter we measure the very prominences, and observe the varieties and inequalities of the surface through our glasses—

"Forests and mountains on her spotted orb.

"But we see nothing in the interior of Africa, but what some compilers of maps or geographers are fanciful enough to imagine. What a happy event, therefore, should we not expect from a voyage of discovery and colonization undertaken in so magnificent a style as the present! what a pride—what an acquisition to philosophy!"

CHAPTER XXV

Count Gosamer thrown by Sphinx into the snow on the top of Teneriffe—Gog and Magog conduct Sphinx for the rest of the voyage—The Baron arrives at the Cape, and unites his former chariot, &c., to his new retinue—Passes into Africa, proceeding from the Cape northwards—Defeats a host of lions by a curious stratagem—Travels through an immense desert—His whole company, chariot, &c., overwhelmed by a whirlwind of sand—Extricates them, and arrives in a fertile country.

THE BRAVE COUNT GOSAMER, WITH A PAIR OF hell-fire spurs on, riding upon Sphinx, directed the whole retinue towards the Madeiras. But the Count had no small share of an amiable vanity, and perceiving great multitudes of people, Gascons, &c., assembled upon the French coast, he could not refrain from showing some singular capers, such as they had never seen before: but especially when he observed all the members of the National Assembly extend themselves along the shore, as a piece of French politeness, to honour this expedition, with Rousseau, Voltaire, and Beelzebub at their head; he set spurs to Sphinx, and at the same time cut and cracked away as hard as he could, holding in the reins with all his might, striving to make the creature plunge and show some uncommon diversion. But sulky and ill-tempered was Sphinx at the time: she plunged indeed—such a devil of a plunge, that she dashed him in one jerk over her head, and he fell precipitately into the water before her. It was in the Bay of Biscay, all the world knows a very boisterous sea, and Sphinx fearing he would be drowned, never turned to the left or the right out of her way, but advancing furious, just stooped her head a little, and supped the poor count off the water, into her mouth, to- gether with the quantity of two or three tuns of water, which she must have taken in along with him, but which were, to such an enormous creature as Sphinx, nothing more than a spoonful would be to any of you or me. She swallowed him, but when she had got him in her stom- ach, his long spurs so scratched and tickled her, that they produced the effect of an emetic. No sooner was he in, but out he was squirted with the most horrible impetu- osity, like a ball or a shell from the calibre of a mortar. Sphinx was at this time quite seasick, and the unfortu- nate count was driven forth like a skyrocket, and landed upon the peak of Teneriffe, plunged over head and ears in the snow—*requiescat in pace!*

I perceived all this mischief from my seat in the ark, but was in such a convulsion of laughter that I could not utter an intelligible word. And now Sphinx, deprived of her postillion, went on in a zigzag direction, and gam- bolled away after a most dreadful manner. And thus had everything gone to wreck, had I not given instant orders to Gog and Magog to sally forth. They plunged into the water, and swimming on each side, got at length right before the animal, and then seized the reins. Thus they continued swimming on each side, like tritons, holding the muzzle of Sphinx, while I, sallying forth astride upon the creature's back, steered forward on our voyage to the Cape of Good Hope.

Arriving at the Cape, I immediately gave orders to repair my former chariot and machines, which were very expeditiously performed by the excellent artists I had brought with me from Europe. And now everything being refitted, we launched forth upon the water: perhaps there never was anything seen more glorious or more august. 'Twas magnificent to behold Sphinx make her obeisance on the water, and the crickets chirp upon the bulls in return of the salute; while Gog and Magog advancing, took the reins of the great John Mowmowsky, and leading towards us chariot and all, instantly disposed of them to the forepart of the ark by hooks and eyes, and tackled Sphinx before all the bulls. Thus the whole had a most tremendous and triumphal appearance. In front floated forwards the mighty Sphinx, with Gog and Magog on each side; next followed in order the bulls with crickets upon their heads; and then advanced the chariot of Queen Mab, containing the curious seat and orrery of heaven; after which appeared the boat and ark of council, overtopped with two balloons, which gave an air of greater lightness and elegance to the whole. I placed in the galleries under the balloons, and on the backs of the bulls, a number of excellent vocal performers, with martial music of clarionets and trumpets. They sung the "Watery Dangers," and the "Pomp of Deep Cerulean!" The sun shone glorious on the water while the procession advanced toward the land, under five hundred arches of ice, illuminated with coloured lights, and adorned in the most grotesque and fanciful style with sea-weed,

elegant festoons, and shells of every kind; while a thousand water-spouts danced eternally before and after us,
attracting the water from the sea in a kind of cone, and
suddenly uniting with the most fantastical thunder and
lightning.

Having landed our whole retinue, we immediately
began to proceed toward the heart of Africa, but first
thought it expedient to place a number of wheels under
the ark for its greater facility of advancing. We journeyed
nearly due north for several days, and met with nothing
remarkable except the astonishment of the savage natives
to behold our equipage.

The Dutch Government at the Cape, to do them justice, gave us every possible assistance for the expedition.
I presume they had received instruction on that head
from their High Mightinesses in Holland. However,
they presented us with a specimen of some of the most
excellent of their Cape wine, and showed us every politeness in their power. As to the face of the country, as we
advanced, it appeared in many places capable of every
cultivation, and of abundant fertility. The natives and
Hottentots of this part of Africa have been frequently
described by travellers, and therefore it is not necessary
to say any more about them. But in the more interior
parts of Africa the appearance, manners, and genius of
the people are totally different.

We directed our course by the compass and the
stars, getting every day prodigious quantities of game
in the woods, and at night encamping within a proper
enclosure for fear of the wild beasts. One whole day in
particular we heard on every side, among the hills, the
horrible roaring of lions, resounding from rock to rock

like broken thunder. It seemed as if there was a general rendezvous of all these savage animals to fall upon our party. That whole day we advanced with caution, our hunters scarcely venturing beyond pistol shot from the caravan for fear of dissolution. At night we encamped as usual, and threw up a circular entrenchment round our tents. We had scarce retired to repose when we found ourselves serenaded by at least one thousand lions, approaching equally on every side, and within a hundred paces. Our cattle showed the most horrible symptoms of fear, all trembling, and in cold perspiration. I directly ordered the whole company to stand to their arms, and not to make any noise by firing till I should command them. I then took a large quantity of tar, which I had brought with our caravan for that purpose, and strewed it in a continued stream round the encampment, within which circle of tar I immediately placed another train or circle of gunpowder, and having taken this precaution, I anxiously waited the lions' approach. These dreadful animals, knowing, I presume, the force of our troop, advanced very slowly, and with caution, approaching on every side of us with an equal pace, and growling in hideous concert, so as to resemble an earthquake, or some similar convulsion of the world. When they had at length advanced and steeped all their paws in the tar, they put their noses to it, smelling it as if it were blood, and daubed their great bushy hair and whiskers with it equal to their paws. At that very instant, when, in concert, they were to give the mortal dart upon us, I discharged a pistol at the train of gunpowder, which instantly exploded on every side, made all the lions recoil in general uproar, and take to flight with the utmost precipitation. In an instant we could behold them scattered through the woods at some distance, roaring in agony, and moving about like so many Will-o'-the-Wisps, their paws and faces all on fire from the tar and the gunpowder. I then ordered a general pursuit: we followed them on every side through the woods, their own light serving as our guide, until, before the rising of the sun, we followed into their fastnesses and shot or otherwise destroyed every one of them, and during the whole of our journey after we never heard the roaring of a lion, nor did any wild beast presume to make another attack upon our party, which shows the excellence of immediate presence of mind, and the terror inspired into the most savage enemies by a proper and well-timed proceeding.

We at length arrived on the confines of an immeasurable desert—an immense plain, extending on every side of us like an ocean. Not a tree, nor a shrub, nor a blade of grass was to be seen, but all appeared an extreme fine sand, mixed with gold-dust and little sparkling pearls.

The gold-dust and pearls appeared to us of little value, because we could have no expectation of returning to England for a considerable time. We observed, at a great distance, something like a smoke arising just over the verge of the horizon, and looking with our telescopes we perceived it to be a whirlwind tearing up the sand and tossing it about in the heavens with frightful impetuosity. I immediately ordered my company to erect a mound around us of a great size, which we did with astonishing labour and perseverance, and then roofed it over with certain planks and timber, which we had with us for the purpose. Our labour was scarcely finished when the sand came rolling in like the waves of the sea; 'twas a storm and river of sand united. It continued to advance in the same direction, without intermission, for three days, and completely covered over the mound we had erected, and buried us all within. The intense heat of the place was intolerable; but guessing, by the cessation of the noise, that

the storm was passed, we set about digging a passage to the light of day again, which we effected in a very short time, and ascending, perceived that the whole had been so completely covered with the sand, that there appeared no hills, but one continued plain, with inequalities or ridges on it like the waves of the sea. We soon extricated our vehicle and retinue from the burning sands, but not without great danger, as the heat was very violent, and began to proceed on our voyage. Storms of sand of a similar nature several times attacked us, but by using the same precautions we preserved ourselves repeatedly from destruction. Having travelled more than nine thousand miles over this inhospitable plain, exposed to the perpendicular rays of a burning sun, without ever meeting a rivulet, or a shower from heaven to refresh us, we at length became almost desperate, when, to our inexpressible joy, we beheld some mountains at a great distance, and on our nearer approach observed them covered with a carpet of verdure and groves and woods. Nothing could appear more romantic or beautiful than the rocks and precipices intermingled with flowers and shrubs of every kind, and palm-trees of such a prodigious size as to surpass anything ever seen in Europe. Fruits of all kinds appeared growing wild in the utmost abundance, and antelopes and sheep and buffaloes wandered about the groves and valleys in profusion. The trees resounded with the melody of birds, and everything displayed a general scene of rural happiness and joy.

CHAPTER XXVI

A feast on live bulls and kava—The inhabitants admire the European adventurers—The Emperor comes to meet the Baron, and pays him great compliments—The inhabitants of the centre of Africa descended from the people of the moon proved by an inscription in Africa, and by the analogy of their language, which is also the same with that of the ancient Scythians—The Baron is declared sovereign of the interior of Africa on the decease of the Emperor—He endeavours to abolish the custom of eating live bulls, which excites much discontent—The advice of Hilaro Frosticos upon the occasion—The Baron makes a speech to an Assembly of the states, which only excites greater murmurs—He consults with Hilaro Frosticos.

HAVING PASSED OVER THE NEAREST MOUNTAINS we entered a delightful vale where we perceived a multitude of persons at a feast of living bulls, whose flesh they cut away with great knives, making a table of the creature's carcase, serenaded by the bellowing of the unfortunate animal. Nothing seemed requisite to add to the barbarity of this feast but *kava*, made as described in Cook's voyages, and at the conclusion of the feast we perceived them brewing this liquor, which they drank with the utmost avidity. From that moment, inspired with an idea of universal benevolence, I determined to abolish the custom of eating live flesh and drinking of kava. But I knew that such a thing could not be immediately effected, whatever in future time might be performed.

Having rested ourselves during a few days, we determined to set out towards the principal city of the empire. The singularity of our appearance was spoken of all over the country as a phenomenon. The multitude looked upon Sphinx, the bulls, the crickets, the balloons, and the whole company, as something more than terrestrial, but especially the thunder of our fire-arms, which struck horror and amazement into the whole nation.

We at length arrived at the metropolis, situated on the banks of a noble river, and the emperor, attended by all his court, came out in grand procession to meet us. The emperor appeared mounted on a dromedary, royally caparisoned, with all his attendants on foot through respect for his Majesty. He was rather above the middle stature of that country, four feet three inches in height, with a countenance, like all his countrymen, as white as snow! He was preceded by a band of most exquisite music, according to the fashion of the country, and his whole retinue halted within about fifty paces of our troop. We returned the salute by a discharge of musketry, and a flourish of our trumpets and martial music. I commanded our caravan to halt, and dismounting, advanced uncovered, with only two attendants, towards his Majesty. The emperor was equally polite, and descending from his dromedary, advanced to meet me. "I am happy," said he, "to have the honour to receive so illustrious a traveller, and assure you that everything in my empire shall be at your disposal."

I thanked his Majesty for his politeness, and expressed how happy I was to meet so polished and refined a people in the centre of Africa, and that I hoped to show myself and company grateful for his esteem, by introducing the arts and sciences of Europe among the people.

I immediately perceived the true descent of this people, which does not appear of terrestrial origin, but descended from some of the inhabitants of the moon, because the principal language spoken there, and in the centre of Africa, is very nearly the same. Their alphabet and method of writing are pretty much the same, and show the extreme antiquity of this people, and their exalted origin. I here give you a specimen of their writing [*Vide Otrckocsus de Orig. Hung. p.46*]: —Sregnah, dna skoohtop.

These characters I have submitted to the inspection of a celebrated antiquarian, and it will be proved to the satisfaction of every one, in his next volume, what an immediate intercourse there must have been between the inhabitants of the moon and the ancient Scythians, which Scythians did not by any means inhabit a part of Russia, but the central part of Africa, as I can abundantly prove to my very learned and laborious friend. The above words, written in our characters, are *Sregnah dna skoohtop*; that is, The Scythians are of heavenly origin. The word *Sregnah* which signifies Scythians, is compounded of *sreg* or *sre*, whence our present English word sire, or sir: and *nah*, or *gnah*, knowledge, because the Scythians united the essentials of nobility and learning together: *dna* signifies heaven, or belonging to the moon, from *duna*, who was anciently worshipped as goddess of that luminary. And *skoohtop* signifies the origin or beginning of anything, from *skoo*, the name used in the moon for a point in geometry, and *top* or *htop*, vegetation. These words are inscribed at this day upon a pyramid in the centre of Africa, nearly at the source of the river Niger; and if any one refuses his assent, he may go there to be convinced.

The emperor conducted me to his court amidst the admiration of his courtiers, and paid us every possible politeness that African magnificence could bestow. He never presumed to proceed on any expedition without consulting us, and looking upon us as a species of superior beings, paid the greatest respect to our opinions. He frequently asked me about the states of Europe, and the kingdom of Great Britain, and appeared lost in admiration at the account I gave him of our shipping, and the immensity of the ocean. We taught him to regulate the government nearly on the same plan with the British constitution, and to institute a parliament and degrees of nobility. His majesty was the last of his royal line, and on his decease, with the unanimous consent of the people, made me heir to the whole empire. The nobility and chiefs of the country immediately waited upon me with petitions, entreating me to accept the government. I consulted with my noble friends, Gog and Magog, &c., and after much consultation it was agreed that I should accept the government, not as actual and independent monarch of the place, but as viceroy to his Majesty of England.

I now thought it high time to do away the custom of eating of live flesh and drinking of kava, and for that purpose used every persuasive method to wean the majority of the people from it. This, to my astonishment, was not taken in good part by the nation, and they looked with jealousy at those strangers who wanted to make innovations among them.

Nevertheless, I felt much concern to think that my fellow-creatures could be capable of such barbarity. I did everything that a heart fraught with universal benevolence and good will to all mankind could be capable of desiring. I first tried every method of persuasion and incitement. I did not harshly reprove them, but I invited frequently whole thousands to dine, after the fashion of Europe, upon roasted meat. Alas, 'twas all in vain! my goodness nearly excited a sedition. They murmured among themselves, spoke of my intentions, my wild and ambitious views, as if I, O heaven! could have had any personal interested motive in making them live like men, rather than like crocodiles and tigers. In fine, perceiving that gentleness could be of no avail, well knowing that when complaisance can effect nothing from some spirits, compulsion excites respect and veneration, I prohibited, under the pain of the severest penalties, the drinking of kava, or eating of live flesh, for the space of nine days, within the districts of Angalinar and Paphagalna.

But this created such an universal abhorrence and detestation of my government, that my ministers, and even myself, were universally pasquinadoed; lampoons, satires, ridicule, and insult, were showered upon the name of Munchausen wherever it was mentioned; and in fine, there never was a government so much detested, or with such little reason.

In this dilemma I had recourse to the advice of my noble friend Hilaro Frosticos. In his good sense I now expected some resource, for the rest of the council, who had advised me to the former method, had given but a poor specimen of their abilities and discernment, or I should have succeeded more happily. In snort, he addressed himself to me and to the council as follows:—

"It is in vain, most noble Munchausen, that your Excellency endeavours to compel or force these people to a life to which they have never been accustomed. In vain do you tell them that apple-pies, pudding, roast beef, minced pies, or tarts, are delicious, that sugar is sweet, that wine is exquisite. Alas! they cannot, they will not comprehend what deliciousness is, what sweetness, or what the flavour of the grape. And even if they were convinced of the superior excellence of your way of life, never, never would they be persuaded; and that if for no other reason, but because force or persuasion is employed to induce them to it. Abandon that idea for the present, and let us try another method. My opinion, therefore, is, that we should at once cease all endeavours to compel or persuade them. But let us, if possible, procure a quantity of fudge from England, and carelessly scatter it over all the country; and from this disposal of matters I presume—nay, I have a moral certainty, that we shall reclaim this people from horror and barbarity."

Had this been proposed at any other time, it would have been violently opposed in the council; but now, when every other attempt had failed, when there seemed no other resource, the majority willingly submitted to they knew not what, for they absolutely had no idea of the manner, the possibility of success, or how they could bring matters to bear. However, 'twas a scheme, and as such they submitted. For my part, I listened with ecstasy to the words of Hilaro Frosticos, for I knew that he had a most singular knowledge of human kind, and could humour and persuade them on to their own happiness and universal good. Therefore, according to the advice of Hilaro, I despatched a balloon with four men over the desert to the Cape of Good Hope, with letters to be forwarded to England, requiring, without delay, a few cargoes of fudge.

The people had all this time remained in a general state of ferment and murmur. Everything that rancour, low wit, and deplorable ignorance could conceive to asperse my government, was put in execution. The most worthy, even the most beneficent actions, everything that was amiable, were perverted into opposition.

The heart of Munchausen was not made of such impenetrable stuff as to be insensible to the hatred of even the most worthless wretch in the whole kingdom; and once, at a general assembly of the states, filled with an idea of such continued ingratitude, I spoke as pathetic as possible, not, methought, beneath my dignity, to make them feel for me: that the universal good and happiness of the people were all I wished or desired; that if my actions had been mistaken, or improper surmises formed, still I had no wish, no desire, but the public welfare, &c. &c. &c.

Hilaro Frosticos was all this time much disturbed;

he looked sternly at me—he frowned, but I was so engrossed with the warmth of my heart, my intentions, that
I understood him not: in a minute I saw nothing but as
if through a cloud (such is the force of amiable sensibil-
ity)—lords, ladies, chiefs—the whole assembly seemed to
swim before my sight. The more I thought on my good
intentions, the lampoons which so much affected my delicacy, good nature, tenderness—I forgot myself—I spoke
rapid, violent—beneficence—fire—tenderness—alas! I
melted into tears!

"Pish! pish!" said Hilaro Frosticos.

Now, indeed, was my government lampooned, sati-
rized, carribonadoed, bepickled, and bedevilled. One
day, with my arm full of lampoons, I started up as Hilaro
entered the room, the tears in my eyes: "Look, look here
Hilaro!—how can I bear all this? It is impossible to please
them; I will leave the government—I cannot bear it! See
what pitiful anecdotes—what surmises: I will make my
people feel for me—I will leave the government!"

"Pshaw!" says Hilaro. At that simple monosyllable I
found myself changed as if by magic! for I ever looked
on Hilaro as a person so experienced—such fortitude,
such good sense. "There are three sail, under the convoy of a frigate," added Hilaro, "just arrived at the Cape,
after a fortunate passage, laden with the fudge that we
demanded. No time is to be lost; let it be immediately
conducted hither, and distributed through the principal
granaries of the empire."

CHAPTER XXVII

A proclamation by the Baron—Excessive curiosity of the people to know what fudge was—The people in a general ferment about it—They break open all the granaries in the empire— The affections of the people conciliated—An ode performed in honour of the Baron—His discourse with Fragrantia on the excellence of the music.

SOME TIME AFTER I ORDERED THE FOLLOWING proclamation to be published in the Court Gazette, and in all the other papers of the empire:—

BY THE MOST MIGHTY AND PUISSANT LORD,
HIS EXCELLENCY THE
LORD BARON MUNCHAUSEN.

WHEREAS a quantity of fudge has been distributed through all the granaries of the empire for particular uses; and as the natives have ever expressed their aversion to all manner of European eatables, it is hereby strictly forbidden, under pain of the severest penalties, for any of the officers charged with the keeping of the said fudge to give, sell, or suffer to be sold, any part or quantity whatever of the said material, until it be agreeable unto our good will and pleasure.

MUNCHAUSEN.

Dated in our Castle of Gristariska
    this Triskill of the month of
    Griskish, in the year Moulikasra-
    navas-kashna-vildash.

This proclamation excited the most ardent curiosity all over the empire. "Do you know what this fudge is?" said Lady Mooshilgarousti to Lord Darnarlaganl. "Fudge!" said he, "Fudge! no: what fudge?" "I mean," replied her Ladyship, "the enormous quantity of fudge that has been distributed under guards in all the strong places in the empire, and which is strictly forbidden to be sold or given to any of the natives under the severest penalties." "Lord!" replied he, "what in the name of wonder can it be? Forbidden! why it must, but pray do you, Lady Fashashash, do you know what this fudge is? Do you, Lord Trastillauex? or you, Miss Gristilarkask? What! nobody know what this fudge can be?"

It engrossed for several days the chit-chat of the whole empire. Fudge, fudge, fudge, resounded in all companies and in all places, from the rising until the setting of the sun; and even at night, when gentle sleep refreshed the rest of mortals, the ladies of all that country were dreaming of fudge!

"Upon my honour," said Kitty, as she was adjusting her modesty piece before the glass, just after getting out of bed, "there is scarce anything I would not give to know what this fudge can be." "La! my dear," replied Miss Killnariska, "I have been dreaming the whole night of

nothing but fudge; I thought my lover kissed my hand, and pressed it to his bosom while I, frowning, endeavoured to wrest it from him: that he kneeled at my feet. No, never, never will I look at you, cried I, till you tell me what this fudge can be, or get me some of it. Begone! cried I, with all the dignity of offended beauty, majesty, and a tragic queen. Begone! never see me more, or bring me this delicious fudge. He swore, on the honour of a knight, that he would wander o'er the world, encounter every danger, perish in the attempt, or satisfy the angel of his soul."

The chiefs and nobility of the nation, when they met together to drink their kava, spoke of nothing but fudge. Men, women, and children all, all talked of nothing but fudge. 'Twas a fury of curiosity, one general ferment, an universal fever—nothing but fudge could allay it.

But in one respect they all agreed, that government must have had some interested view in giving such positive orders to preserve it, and keep it from the natives of the country. Petitions were addressed to me from all quarters, from every corporation and body of men in the whole empire. The majority of the people instructed their constituents, and the parliament presented a petition, praying that I would be pleased to take the state of the nation under consideration, and give orders to satisfy the people, or the most dreadful consequences were to be apprehended. To these requests, at the entreaty of my council, I made no reply, or at best but unsatisfactory answers. Curiosity was on the rack; they forgot to lampoon the government, so engaged were they about the fudge. The great assembly of the states could think of nothing else. Instead of enacting laws for the regulation of the people, instead of consulting what should seem most wise, most excellent, they could think, talk, and harangue of nothing but fudge. In vain did the Speaker call to order; the more checks they got the more extravagant and inquisitive they were.

In short, the populace in many places rose in the most outrageous and tumultuous manner, forced open the granaries in all places in one day, and triumphantly distributed the fudge through the whole empire.

Whether on account of the longing, the great curiosity, imagination, or the disposition of the people, I cannot say—but they found it infinitely to their taste; 'twas an intoxication of joy, satisfaction, and applause.

Finding how much they liked this fudge, I procured another quantity from England, much greater than the former, and cautiously bestowed it over all the kingdom. Thus were the affections of the people regained; and they, from hence, began to venerate, applaud, and admire my government more than ever. The following ode was performed at the castle, in the most superb style, and universally admired:—

ODE.

Ye bulls and crickets, and Gog, Magog,
And trump'ts high chiming anthrophog,
Come sing blithe choral all in *og*,
Caralog, basilog, fog, and bog!

Great and superb appears thy cap sublime,
　　Admired and worshipp'd as the rising sun;

Solemn, majestic, wise, like hoary Time,
  And fam'd alike for virtue, sense, and fun.

Then swell the noble strain with song,
  And elegance divine,
While goddesses around shall throng,
  And all the muses nine.

And bulls, and crickets, and Gog, Magog,
And trumpets chiming anthrophog,
Shall sing blithe choral all in *og*,
Caralog, basilog, fog, and bog!

This piece of poetry was much applauded, admired
and *encored* in every public assembly, celebrated as an
astonishing effort of genius; and the music, composed by
Minheer Gastrashbark Gkrghhbarwskhk, was thought
equal to the sense!—Never was there anything so universally admired, the summit of the most exquisite wit, the
keenest praise, the most excellent music.

"Upon my honour, and the faith I owe my love," said
I, "music may be talked of in England, but to possess
the very soul of harmony the world should come to the

performance of this ode." Lady Fragrantia was at that moment drumming with her fingers on the edge of her fan, lost in a reverie, thinking she was playing upon—— Was it a forte piano?

"No, my dear Fragrantia," said I, tenderly taking her in my arms while she melted into tears; "never, never, will I play upon any other——!"

Oh! 'twas divine, to see her like a summer's morning, all blushing and full of dew!

CHAPTER XXVIII

The Baron sets all the people of the empire to work to build a bridge from their country to Great Britain—His contrivance to render the arch secure—Orders an inscription to be engraved on the bridge—Returns with all his company, chariot, etc., to England—Surveys the kingdoms and nations under him from the middle of the bridge.

"AND NOW, MOST NOBLE BARON," SAID THE illustrious Hilaro Frosticos, "now is the time to make this people proceed in any business that we find convenient. Take them at this present ferment of the mind, let them not think, but at once set them to work." In short, the whole nation went heartily to the business, to build an edifice such as was never seen in any other country. I took care to supply them with their favourite kava and fudge, and they worked like horses. The tower of Babylon, which, according to Hermogastricus, was seven miles high, or the Chinese wall, was a mere trifle, in comparison to this stupendous edifice, which was completed in a very short space of time.

It was of an immense height, far beyond anything that ever had been before erected, and of such gentle ascent, that a regiment of cavalry with a train of cannon could

ascend with perfect ease and facility. It seemed like a rainbow in the heavens, the base of which appeared to rise in
the centre of Africa, and the other extremity seemed to
stoop into Great Britain. A most noble bridge indeed,
and a piece of masonry that has outdone Sir Christopher Wren. Wonderful must it have been to form so
tremendous an arch, especially as the artists had certain
difficulties to labour against which they could not have
in the formation of any other arch in the world—I mean,
the attraction of the moon and planets: Because the arch
was of so great a height, and in some parts so elongated
from the earth, as in a great measure to diminish in its
gravitation to the centre of our globe; or rather, seemed
more easily operated upon by the attraction of the planets: So that the stones of the arch, one would think, at
certain times, were ready to fall *up* to the moon, and at
other times to fall down to the earth. But as the former
was more to be dreaded, I secured stability to the fabric
by a very curious contrivance: I ordered the architects to
get the heads of some hundred numbskulls and block-
heads, and fix them to the interior surface of the arch, at
certain intervals, all the whole length, by which means
the arch was held together firm, and its inclination to
the earth eternally established; because of all the things
in the world, the skulls of these kind of animals have a
strange facility of tending to the centre of the earth.

The building being completed, I caused an inscription to be engraved in the most magnificent style upon
the summit of the arch, in letters so great and luminous,
that all vessels sailing to the East or West Indies might
read them distinct in the heavens, like the motto of
Constantine.

KARDOL BAGARLAN KAI TON FARINGO SARGAI RA
MO PASHROL VATINEAC CAL COLNITOS RO NA FIL-
NAT AGASTRA SA DINGANNAL FANO.

That is to say, "As long as this arch and bond of union
shall exist, so long shall the people be happy. Nor can
all the power of the world affect them, unless the moon,
advancing from her usual sphere, should so much attract
the skulls as to cause a sudden elevation, on which the
whole will fall into the most horrible confusion."

An easy intercourse being thus established between
Great Britain and the centre of Africa, numbers travelled
continually to and from both countries, and at my request mail coaches were ordered to run on the bridge
between both empires. After some time, having settled
the government perfectly to my satisfaction, I requested
permission to resign, as a great cabal had been excited
against me in England; I therefore received my letters of
recall, and prepared to return to Old England.

In fine, I set out upon my journey, covered with applause and general admiration. I proceeded with the
same retinue that I had before—Sphinx, Gog and Magog, &c., and advanced along the bridge, lined on each
side with rows of trees, adorned with festoons of various flowers, and illuminated with coloured lights. We
advanced at a great rate along the bridge, which was so
very extensive that we could scarcely perceive the ascent,
but proceeded insensibly until we arrived on the centre
of the arch. The view from thence was glorious beyond
conception; 'twas divine to look down on the kingdoms
and seas and islands under us. Africa seemed in general of a tawny brownish colour, burned up by the sun:

Spain seemed more inclining to a yellow, on account of
some fields of corn scattered over the kingdom; France
appeared more inclining
to a bright straw-colour,
intermixed with green;
and England appeared
covered with the most
beautiful verdure. I ad-
mired the appearance
of the Baltic Sea, which
evidently seemed to have
been introduced be-
tween those countries by
the sudden splitting of
the land, and that origi-
nally Sweden was united
to the western coast of
Denmark; in short, the
whole interstice of the

Gulf of Finland had no being, until these countries, by
mutual consent, separated from one another. Such were
my philosophical meditations as I advanced, when I observed a man in armour, with a tremendous spear or
lance, and mounted upon a steed, advancing against me.
I soon discovered by a telescope that it could be no other
than Don Quixote, and promised myself much amusement in the rencounter.

CHAPTER XXIX

The Baron's retinue is opposed in a heroic style by Don Quixote, who in his turn is attacked by Gog and Magog—Lord Whittington, with the Lord Mayor's show, comes to the assistance of Don Quixote—Gog and Magog assail his Lordship—Lord Whittington makes a speech, and deludes Gog and Magog to his party—A general scene of uproar and battle among the company, until the Baron, with great presence of mind, appeases the tumult.

"WHAT ART THOU?" EXCLAIMED DON QUIXOTE on his potent steed. "Who art thou? Speak! or, by the eternal vengeance of mine arm, thy whole machinery shall perish at sound of this my trumpet!"

Astonished at so rude a salutation, the great Sphinx stopped short, and bridling up herself, drew in her head, like a snail when it touches something that it does not like: the bulls set up a horrid bellowing, the crickets sounded an alarm, and Gog and Magog advanced before the rest. One of these powerful brothers had in his hand a great pole, to the extremity of which was fastened a cord of about two feet in length, and to the end of the cord was fastened a ball of iron, with spikes shooting from it like the rays of a star; with this weapon he prepared to encounter, and advancing thus he spoke:—

"Audacious wight! that thus, in complete steel arrayed, doth dare to venture cross my way, to stop the great Munchausen. Know then, proud knight, that thou shalt instant perish 'neath my potent arm."

When Quixote, Mancha's knight, responded firm:—

"Gigantic monster! leader of witches, crickets, and chimeras dire! know thou, that here before yon azure heaven the cause of truth, of valour, and of faith right pure shall ordeal counter try it!"

Thus he spoke, and brandishing his mighty spear, would instant prodigies sublime performed, had not some wight placed 'neath the tail of dark Rosinante furze all thorny base; at which, quadrupedanting, plunged the steed, and instant on the earth the knight roared *credo* for his life.

At that same moment ten thousand frogs started from the morions of Gog and Magog, and furiously assailed the knight on every side. In vain he roared, and invoked fair Dulcinea del Toboso: for frogs' wild croaking seemed more loud, more sonorous than all his invocations. And thus in battle vile the knight was overcome, and spawn all swarmed upon his glittering helmet.

"Detested miscreants!" roared the knight; "avaunt! Enchanters dire and goblins could alone this arduous task perform; to rout the knight of Mancha, foul defeat, and war, even such as ne'er was known before. Then hear, O del Toboso! hear my vows, that thus in anguish of my soul I urge, 'midst frogs, Gridalbin, Hecaton, Kai, Talon, and the Rove! [for such the names and definitions of their qualities, their separate powers.] For Merlin plumed their airy flight, and then in watery moonbeam dyed his rod eccentric. At the touch ten thousand frogs, strange metamorphosed, croaked even thus: And here they come, on high behest, to vilify the knight that erst defended famed virginity, and matrons all bewronged, and pilgrims hoar, and courteous guise of all! But the age of chivalry is gone, and the glory of Europe is extinguished for ever?"

He spake, and sudden good Lord Whittington, at head of all his raree-show, came forth, armour antique of chivalry, and helmets old, and troops, all streamers, flags and banners glittering gay, red, gold, and purple; and in every hand a square of gingerbread, all gilded nice, was brandished awful. At a word, ten thousand thousand Naples biscuits, crackers, buns, and flannel-cakes, and hats of gingerbread encountered in mid air in glorious exaltation, like some huge storm of millstones, or when it rains whole clouds of dogs and cats.

The frogs, astonished, thunderstruck, forgot their notes and music, that before had seemed so terrible, and drowned the cries of knight renown, and mute in wonder heard the words of Whittington, pronouncing solemn:—"Goblins, chimeras dire, or frogs, or whatsoe'er enchantment thus presents in antique shape, attend and hear the words of peace; and thou, good herald, read aloud the Riot Act!"

He ceased, and dismal was the tone that softly breathed from all the frogs in chorus, who quick had petrified with fright, unless redoubted Gog and Magog, both with poles, high topped with airy bladders by a string dependent, had not stormed against his lordship. Ever and anon the bladders, loud resounding on his chaps, proclaimed their fury against all potent law, coercive mayoralty; when he, submissive, thus in cunning guile addressed the knights assailant:—"Gog, Magog, renowned and famous! what, my sons, shall you assail your father, friend, and chief confessed? Shall you, thus armed with bladders vile, attack my title, eminence, and pomp sublime? Subside, vile discord, and again return to your true 'legiance. Think, my friends how oft your gorgeous, pouch I've crammed, all calapash, green fat, and calapee. Remember how you've feasted, stood inert for ages, until size immense you've gained. And think, how different is the service of Munchausen, where you o'er seas, cold, briny, float along the tide, eternal toiling like to slaves of Algiers and Tripoli. And ev'n on high, balloon like, through the heavens have journeyed late, upon a rainbow or some awful bridge stretched eminent, as if on earth he had not work sufficient to distress your potent servitudes, but he should also seek in heaven dire cause of labour! Recollect, my friends, even why or wherefore should you thus assail your lawful magistrate, or why desert his livery? or for what or wherefore serve this German Lord Munchausen, who for all your labour shall alone bestow some fudge and heroic blows in war? Then cease, and thus in amity return to friendship aldermanic, bungy, brown, and sober."

Ceased he then, right worshipful, when both the warring champions instant stemmed their battle, and in sign of peace and unity returning, 'neath their feet reclined their weapons. Sudden at a signal either stamped his foot sinistrine, and the loud report of bursten bladder stunned each ear surrounding, like the roar of thunder from on high convulsing heaven and earth.

'Twas now upon the saddle once again the knight of

Mancha rose, and in his hand far balancing his lance,
full tilt against the troops of bulls opposing ran. And
thou, shrill Crillitrilkril, than whom no cricket e'er on
hob of rural cottage, or chimney black, more gladsome
tuned his merry note, e'en thou didst perish, shrieking
gave the ghost in empty air, the sport of every wind; for
e'en that heart so jocund and so gay was pierced, harsh
spitted by the lance of Mancha, while undaunted thou
didst sit between the horns that crowned Mowmowsky.
And now Whittington advanced, 'midst armour antique
and the powers Magog and Gog, and with his rod en-
chanting touched the head of every frog, long mute and
thunderstruck, at which, in universal chorus and salute,
they sung blithe jocund, and amain advanced rebellious
'gainst my troop.

While Sphinx, though great, gigantic, seemed instinctive base and cowardly, and at the sight of storming
gingerbread, and powers, Magog and Gog, and Quixote,
all against her, started fierce, o'erturning boat, balloons,
and all; loud roared the bulls, hideous, and the crash
of wheels, and chaos of confusion drear, resounded far
from earth to heaven. And still more fierce in charge the
great Lord Whittington, from poke of ermine his famed
Grimalkin took. She screamed, and harsh attacked my
bulls confounded; lightning-like she darted, and from
half the troop their eyes devouring tore. Nor could the
riders, crickets throned sublime, escape from rage, from
fury less averse than cannons murder o'er the stormy sea.
The great Mowmowsky roared amain and plunged in anguish, shunning every dart of fire-eyed fierce Grimalkin.
Dire the rage of warfare and contending crickets, Quixote
and great Magog; when Whittington advancing—"Good,

my friends and warriors, headlong on the foe bear down impetuous." He spoke, and waving high the mighty rod, tipped wonderful each bull, at which more fierce the creatures bellowed, while enchantment drear devoured their vitals. And all had gone to wreck in more than mortal strife, unless, like Neptune orient from the stormy deep, I rose, e'en towering o'er the ruins of my fighting troops. Serene and calm I stood, and gazed around undaunted; nor did aught oppose against my foes impetuous. But sudden from chariot purses plentiful of fudge poured forth, and scattered it amain o'er all the crowd contending. As when old Catherine or the careful Joan doth scatter to the chickens bits of bread and crumbs fragmented, while rejoiced they gobble fast the proffered scraps in general plenty and fraternal peace, and "hush," she cries, "hush! hush!"

CHAPTER XXX

The Baron arrives in England—the Colossus of Rhodes comes to congratulate him—Great rejoicings on the Baron's return, and a tremendous concert—The Baron's discourse with Fragrantia, and her opinion of the Tour to the Hebrides

HAVING ARRIVED IN ENGLAND ONCE MORE the greatest rejoicings were made for my return; the whole city seemed one general blaze of illumination, and the Colossus of Rhodes, hearing of my astonishing feats, came on purpose to England to congratulate me on such unparalleled achievements. But above all other rejoicings on my return, the musical oratorio and song of triumph were magnificent in the extreme. Gog and Magog were ordered to take the maiden tower of Windsor, and make a tambourine or great drum of it. For this purpose they extended an elephant's hide, tanned and prepared for the design, across the summit of the tower, from parapet to parapet, so that in proportion this extended elephant's hide was to the whole of the castle what the parchment is to a drum, in such a manner that the whole became one great instrument of war.

To correspond with this, Colossus took Guildhall and Westminster Abbey, and turning the foundations towards the heavens, so that the roofs of the edifices were upon the ground, he strung them across with brass and steel wire from side to side, and thus, when strung, they had the appearance of most noble dulcimers. He then took the great dome of St. Paul's, raising it off the earth with as much facility as you would a decanter of claret. And when once risen up it had the appearance of a quart bottle. Colossus instantly, with his teeth, cracked off the superior part of the cupola, and then applying his lips to the instrument, began to sound it like a trumpet. 'Twas martial, beyond description—*tantara!—tara! —ta!*

During the concert I walked in the park with Lady Fragrantia: she was dressed that morning in a *chemise à la reine.* "I like," said she, "the dew of the morning, 'tis delicate and ethereal, and, by thus bespangling me, I think it will more approximate me to the nature of the rose [for her looks were like Aurora]; and to confirm the vermilion I shall go to Spa." "And drink the Podhon spring?" added I, gazing at her from top to toe. "Yes," replied the lovely Fragrantia, "with all my heart; 'tis the drink of sweetness and delicacy. Never were there any creatures like the water-drinkers at Spa; they seem like so many thirsty blossoms on a peach-tree, that suck up the shower in the scorching heat. There is a certain something in the waters that gives vigour to the whole frame, and expands every heart with rapture and benevolence. They drink! good gods! how they do drink! and then, how they sleep! Pray, my dear Baron, were you ever at the falls of Niagara?" "Yes, my lady," replied I, surprised at such a strange association of ideas; "I have been, many years ago, at the Falls of Niagara, and found no more difficulty in swimming up and down the cataracts than I

should to move a minuet." At that moment she dropped
her nosegay. "Ah," said she, as I presented it to her, "there
is no great variety in these polyanthuses. I do assure you,
my dear Baron, that there is taste in the selection of flowers as well as everything else, and were I a girl of sixteen
I should wear some rosebuds in my bosom, but at five-
and-twenty I think it would be more *apropos* to wear a
full-blown rose, quite ripe, and ready to drop off the stalk
for want of being pulled—heigh-ho!" "But pray, my lady,"
said I, "how do you like the concert?" "Alas!" said she,
languishingly, while she laid her hand upon my shoulder, "what are these bodiless sounds and vibration to me?
and yet what an exquisite sweetness in the songs of the
northern part of our island:—*'Thou art gone awa' from
me, Mary!'* How pathetic and divine the little airs of Scotland and the Hebrides! But never, never can I think of
that same Doctor Johnson—that CONSTABLE, as Fergus
MacLeod calls him—but I have an idea of a great brown
full-bottomed wig and a hogshead of porter! Oh, 'twas
base! to be treated everywhere with politeness and hos-
pitality, and in return invidiously to smellfungus them all
over; to go to the country of Kate of Aberdeen, of Auld
Robin Gray, 'midst rural innocence and sweetness, take
up their plaids, and dance. Oh! Doctor, Doctor!"

"And what would you say, Fragrantia, if you were to
write a tour to the Hebrides?" "Peace to the heroes," replied she, in a delicate and theatrical tone; "peace to the
heroes who sleep in the isle of Iona; the sons of the wave,
and the chiefs of the dark-brown shield! The tear of the
sympathising stranger is scattered by the wind over the
hoary stones as she meditates sorrowfully on the times of
old! Such could I say, sitting upon some druidical heap or

tumulus. The fact is this, there is a right and wrong han-
dle to everything, and there is more pleasure in thinking
with pure nobility of heart, than with the illiberal enmi-
ties and sarcasm of a blackguard."

CHAPTER XXXI

A litigated contention between Don Quixote, Gog, Magog, &c.—A grand court assembled upon it—The appearance of the company—The matrons, judges, &c.—The method of writing, and the use of the fashionable amusement quizzes—Wauwau arrives from the country of Prester John, and leads the whole Assembly a wild-goose chase to the top of Plinlimmon, and thence to Virginia—The Baron meets a floating island in his voyage to America—Pursues Wauwau with his whole company through the deserts of North America—His curious contrivance to seize Wauwau in a morass.

THE CONTENTION BETWEEN GOG AND MAGOG, and Sphinx, Hilaro Frosticos, the Lord Whittington, &c., was productive of infinite litigation. All the lawyers in the kingdom were employed, to render the affair as complex and gloriously uncertain as possible; and, in fine, the whole nation became interested, and were divided on both sides of the question. Colossus took the part of Sphinx, and the affair was at length submitted to the decision of a grand council in a great hall, adorned with seats on every side in form of an amphitheatre. The assembly appeared the most magnificent and splendid in the world. A court or jury of one hundred matrons occupied

the principal and most honourable part of the amphitheatre; they were dressed in flowing robes of sky-blue
velvet adorned with festoons of brilliants and diamond
stars; grave and sedate looking matrons, all in uniform,
with spectacles upon their noses; and opposite to these
were placed one hundred judges, with curly white wigs
flowing down on each side of them to their very feet,
so that Solomon in all his glory was not so wise in appearance. At the ardent request of the whole empire I
condescended to be the president of the court, and being arrayed accordingly, I took my seat beneath a canopy
erected in the centre. Before every judge was placed a
square inkstand, containing a gallon of ink, and pens of
a proportionable size; and also right before him an enormous folio, so large as to serve for table and book at the
same time. But they did not make much use of their pens
and ink, except to blot and daub the paper; for, that they
should be the more impartial, I had ordered that none
but the blind should be honoured with the employment:
so that when they attempted to write anything, they uni-
formly dipped their pens into the machine containing
sand, and having scrawled over a page as they thought,
desiring them to dry it with sand, would spill half a gallon of ink upon the paper, and thereby daubing their
fingers, would transfer the ink to their face whenever
they leaned their cheek upon their hand for greater gravity. As to the matrons, to prevent an eternal prattle that
would drown all manner of intelligibility, I found it absolutely necessary to sew up their mouths; so that between
the blind judges and the dumb matrons methought the
trial had a chance of being terminated sooner than it otherwise would. The matrons, instead of their tongues, had

other instruments to convey their ideas: each of them had three quizzes, one quiz pendant from the string that sewed up her mouth, and another quiz in either hand. When she wished to express her negative, she darted and recoiled the quizzes in her right and left hand; and when she desired to express her affirmative, she, nodding, made the quiz pendant from her mouth flow down and recoil again. The trial proceeded in this manner for a long time, to the admiration of the whole empire, when at length I thought proper to send to my old friend and ally, Prester John, entreating him to forward to me one of the species of wild and curious birds found in his kingdom, called a Wauwau. This creature was brought over the great bridge before mentioned, from the interior of Africa, by a balloon. The balloon was placed upon the bridge, extending over the parapets on each side, with great wings or oars to assist its velocity, and under the balloon was placed pendant a kind of boat, in which were the persons to manage the steerage of the machine, and protect Wauwau. This oracular bird, arriving in England, instantly darted through one of the windows of the great hall, and perched upon the canopy in the centre, to the admiration of all present. Her cackling appeared quite prophetic and oracular; and the first question proposed to her by the unanimous consent of the matrons and judges was, Whether or not the moon was composed of green cheese? The solution of this question was deemed absolutely necessary before they could proceed farther on the trial.

Wauwau seemed in figure not very much differing from a swan, except that the neck was not near so long, and she stood after an admirable fashion like to Vestris.

She began cackling most sonorously, and the whole assembly agreed that it was absolutely necessary to catch her, and having her in their immediate possession, nothing more would be requisite for the termination of this litigated affair. For this purpose the whole house rose up to catch her, and approached in tumult, the judges brandishing their pens, and shaking their big wigs, and the matrons quizzing as much as possible in every direction, which very much startled Wauwau, who, clapping her wings, instantly flew out of the hall. The assembly began to proceed after her in order and style of precedence, together with my whole train of Gog and Magog, Sphinx, Hilaro Frosticos, Queen Mab's chariot, the bulls and crickets, &c., preceded by bands of music; while Wauwau, descending on the earth, ran on like an ostrich before the troop, cackling all the way. Thinking suddenly to catch this ferocious animal, the judges and matrons would suddenly quicken their pace, but the creature would as quickly outrun them, or sometimes fly away for many miles together, and then alight to take breath until we came within sight of her again. Our train journeyed over a most prodigious tract of country in a direct line, over hills and dales, to the summit of Plinlimmon, where we thought to have seized Wauwau; but she instantly took flight, and never ceased until she arrived at the mouth of the Potomac river in Virginia.

Our company immediately embarked in the machines before described, in which we had journeyed into Africa, and after a few days' sail arrived in North America. We met with nothing curious on our voyage, except a floating island, containing some very delightful villages, inhabited by a few whites and negroes; the

sugar cane did not thrive there well, on account, as I was informed, of the variety of the climates; the island being sometimes driven up as far as the north pole, and at other times wafted under the equinoctial. In pity to the poor islanders, I got a huge stake of iron, and driving it through the centre of the island, fastened it to the rocks and mud at the bottom of the sea, since which time the island has become stationary, and is well known at present by the name of St. Christopher's, and there is not an island in the world more secure.

Arriving in North America, we were received by the President of the United States with every honour and politeness. He was pleased to give us all the information possible relative to the woods and immense regions of America, and ordered troops of the different tribes of the Esquimaux to guide us through the forests in pursuit of Wauwau, who, we at length found, had taken refuge in the centre of a morass. The inhabitants of the country, who loved hunting, were much delighted to behold the manner in which we attempted to seize upon Wauwau; the chase was noble and uncommon. I determined to surround the animal on every side, and for this purpose ordered the judges and matrons to surround the morass with nets extending a mile in height, on various parts of which net the company disposed themselves, floating in the air like so many spiders upon their cobwebs. Magog, at my command, put on a kind of armour that he had carried with him for the purpose, corselet of steel, with gauntlets, helmet, &c., so as nearly to resemble a mole. He instantly plunged into the earth, making way with his sharp steel head-piece, and tearing up the ground with his iron claws, and found not much difficulty therein, as

morass in general is of a soft and yielding texture. Thus
he hoped to undermine Wauwau, and suddenly rising,
seize her by the foot, while his brother Gog ascended the
air in a balloon, hoping to catch her if she should escape
Magog. Thus the animal was surrounded on every side,
and at first was very much terrified, knowing not which
way she had best to go. At length hearing an obscure
noise under ground, Wauwau took flight before Magog
could have time to catch her by the foot. She flew to the
right, then to the left, north, east, west, and south, but
found on every side the company prepared upon their
nets. At length she flew right up soaring at a most astonishing rate towards the sun, while the company on
every side set up one general acclamation. But Gog in his
balloon soon stopped Wauwau in the midst of her career,
and snared her in a net, the cords of which he continued to hold in his hand. Wauwau did not totally lose her
presence of mind, but, after a little consideration, made
several violent darts against the volume of the balloon;
so fierce, as at length to tear open a great space, on which
the inflammable air rushing out, the whole apparatus began to tumble to the earth with amazing rapidity. Gog
himself was thrown out of the vehicle, and letting go the
reins of the net, Wauwau got liberty again, and flew out
of sight in an instant.

Gog had been above a mile elevated from the earth
when he began to fall, and as he advanced the rapidity
increased, so that he went like a ball from a cannon into
the morass, and his nose striking against one of the iron-
capped hands of his brother Magog, just then rising from
the depths, he began to bleed violently, and, but for the
softness of the morass, would have lost his life.

CHAPTER XXXII

The Baron harangues the company, and they continue the pursuit—The Baron, wandering from his retinue, is taken by the savages, scalped, and tied to a stake to be roasted; but he contrives to extricate himself, and kills the savages—The Baron travels overland through the forests of North America, to the confines of Russia—Arrives at the castle of the Nareskin Rowskimowmowsky, and gallops into the kingdom of Logger-heads—A battle, in which the Baron fights the Nareskin in single combat, and generously gives him his life—Arrives at the Friendly Islands, and discourses with Omai—The Baron, with all his attendants, goes from Otaheite to the isthmus of Darien, and having cut a canal across the isthmus, returns to England.

"MY FRIENDS, AND VERY LEARNED AND PROFOUND Judiciarii," said I, "be not disheartened that Wauwau has escaped from you at present: persevere, and we shall yet succeed. You should never despair, Munchausen being your general; and therefore be brave, be courageous, and fortune shall second your endeavours. Let us advance undaunted in pursuit, and follow the fierce Wauwau even three times round the globe, until we entrap her."

My words filled them with confidence and valour, and they unanimously agreed to continue the chase.

We penetrated the frightful deserts and gloomy woods of America, beyond the source of the Ohio, through countries utterly unknown before. I frequently took the diversion of shooting in the woods, and one day that I happened with three attendants to wander far from our troop, we were suddenly set upon by a number of savages. As we had expended our powder and shot, and happened to have no sidearms, it was in vain to make any resistance against hundreds of enemies. In short, they bound us, and made us walk before them to a gloomy cavern in a rock, where they feasted upon what game they had killed, but which, not being sufficient, they took my three unfortunate companions and myself, and scalped us. The pain of losing the flesh from my head was most horrible; it made me leap in agonies, and roar like a bull. They then tied us to stakes, and making great fires around us, began to dance in a circle, singing with much distortion and barbarity, and at times putting the palms of their hands to their mouths, set up the war-whoop. As they had on that day also made a great prize of some wine and spirits belonging to our troop, these barbarians, finding it delicious, and unconscious of its intoxicating quality, began to drink it in profusion, while they beheld us roasting, and in a very short time they were all completely drunk, and fell asleep around the fires. Perceiving some hopes, I used most astonishing efforts to extricate myself from the cords with which I was tied, and at length succeeded. I immediately unbound my companions, and though half roasted, they still had power enough to walk. We sought about for the flesh that had been taken off our heads, and having found the scalps, we immediately adapted them to our bloody heads, sticking them on with a kind of glue of a sovereign quality, that flows from a tree in that country, and the parts united and healed in a few hours. We took care to revenge ourselves on the savages, and with their own hatchets put every one of them to death. We then returned to our troop, who had given us up for lost, and they made great rejoicings on our return. We now proceeded in our journey through this prodigious wilderness, Gog and Magog acting as pioneers, hewing down the trees, &c., at a great rate as we advanced. We passed over numberless swamps and lakes and rivers, until at length we discovered a habitation at some distance. It appeared a dark and gloomy castle, surrounded with strong ramparts, and a broad ditch. We called a council of war, and it was determined to send a deputation with a trumpet to the walls of the castle, and demand friend-

ship from the governor, whoever he might be, and an account if aught he knew of Wauwau. For this purpose our whole caravan halted in the wood, and Gog and Magog reclined amongst the trees, that their enormous strength and size should not be discovered, and give umbrage to the lord of the castle. Our embassy approached the castle, and having demanded admittance for some time, at length the drawbridge was let down; and they were suffered to enter. As soon as they had passed the gate it was immediately closed after them, and on either side they perceived ranks of halberdiers, who made them tremble with fear. "We come," the herald proclaimed, "on the part of Hilaro Frosticos, Don Quixote, Lord Whittington, and the thrice-renowned Baron Munchausen, to claim friendship from the governor of

this puissant castle, and to seek Wauwau." "The most noble the governor," replied an officer, "is at all times happy to entertain such travellers as pass through these immense deserts, and will esteem it an honour that the great Hilaro Frosticos, Don Quixote, Lord Whittington, and the thrice-renowned Baron Munchausen, enter his castle walls."

In short, we entered the castle. The governor sat with all our company to table, surrounded by his friends, of a very fierce and warlike appearance. They spoke but little, and seemed very austere and reserved, until the first course was served up. The dishes were brought in by a number of bears walking on their hind-legs, and on every dish was a fricassee of pistols, pistol-bullets, sauce of gun-powder, and aqua-vitae. This entertainment seemed rather indigestible by even an ostrich's stomach, when the governor addressed us, and informed me that it was ever his custom to strangers to offer them for the first course a service similar to that before us: and if they were inclined to accept the invitation, he would fight them as much as they pleased, but if they could not relish the pistol-bullets, &c., he would conclude them peaceable, and try what better politeness he could show them in his castle. In short, the first course being removed untouched, we dined, and after dinner the governor forced the company to push the bottle about with alacrity and to excess. He informed us that he was the Nareskin Rowskimowmowsky, who had retired amidst these wilds, disgusted with the court of Petersburgh. I was rejoiced to meet him; I recollected my old friend, whom I had known at the court of Russia, when I rejected the hand of the Empress. The Nareskin, with all his knights-companions, drank to an astonishing degree, and we all set off upon hobby horses in full cry out of the castle. Never was there seen such a cavalcade before. In front galloped a hundred knights belonging to the castle, with hunting horns and a pack of excellent dogs; and then came the Nareskin Rowskimowmowsky, Gog and Magog, Hilaro Frosticos, and your humble servant, hallooing and shouting like so many demoniacs, and spurring our hobby horses at an infernal rate until we arrived in the kingdom of Loggerheads. The kingdom of Loggerheads was wilder than any part of Siberia, and the Nareskin had here built a romantic summerhouse in a Gothic taste, to which he would frequently retire with his company after dinner. The Nareskin had a dozen bears of enormous stature that danced for our amusement, and their chiefs performed the *minuet de la cour* to admiration. And here the most noble Hilaro Frosticos thought proper to ask the Nareskin some intelligence about Wauwau, in quest of whom we had travelled over such a tract of country, and encountered so many dangerous adventures, and also invited the Nareskin Rowskimowmowsky to attend us with all his bears in the expedition. The Nareskin appeared astonished at the idea; he looked with infinite hauteur and ferocity on Hilaro, and affecting a violent passion, asked him, "Did he imagine that the Nareskin Rowskimowmowsky could condescend to take notice of a Wauwau, let her fly what way she would? Or did he think a chief possessing such blood in his veins could engage in such a foreign pursuit? By the blood of all the bears in the kingdom of Loggerheads, and by the ashes of my great great grandmother, I would cut off your head!"

Hilaro Frosticos resented this oration, and in short a general riot commenced. The bears, together with the hundred knights, took the part of the Nareskin, and Gog and Magog, Don Quixote, the Sphinx, Lord Whittington, the bulls, the crickets, the judges, the matrons, and Hilaro Frosticos, made noble warfare against them.

I drew my sword, and challenged the Nareskin to single combat. He frowned, while his eyes sparkled fire and indignation, and bracing a buckler on his left arm, he advanced against me. I made a blow at him with all my force, which he received upon his buckler, and my sword broke short.

Ungenerous Nareskin! seeing me disarmed, he still pushed forward, dealing his blows upon me with the utmost violence, which I parried with my shield and the hilt of my broken sword, and fought like a game-cock.

An enormous bear at the same time attacked me, but I ran my hand still retaining the hilt of my broken sword down his throat, and tore up his tongue by the roots. I then seized his carcase by the hind-legs, and whirling it over my head, gave the Nareskin such a blow with his own bear as evidently stunned him. I repeated my blows, knocking the bear's head against the Nareskin's head, until, by one happy blow, I got his head into the bear's jaws, and the creature being still somewhat alive and convulsive, the teeth closed upon him like nutcrackers. I threw the bear from me, but the Nareskin remained sprawling, unable to extricate his head from the bear's jaws, imploring for mercy. I gave the wretch his life: a lion preys not upon carcases.

At the same time my troop had effectually routed the bears and the rest of their adversaries. I was merciful, and ordered quarter to be given.

At that moment I perceived Wauwau flying at a great height through the heavens, and we instantly set out in pursuit of her, and never stopped until we arrived at Kamschatka; thence we passed to Otaheite. I met my old acquaintance Omai, who had been in England with the great navigator, Cook, and I was glad to find he had established Sunday schools over all the islands. I talked to him of Europe, and his former voyage to England. "Ah!" said he, most emphatically, "the English, the cruel English, to

murder me with goodness, and refine upon my torture—
took me to Europe, and showed me the court of England,
the delicacy of exquisite life: they showed me gods, and
showed me heaven, as if on purpose to make me feel the
loss of them."

From these islands we set out, attended by a fleet of
canoes with fighting-stages and the chiefest warriors of
the islands, commanded by Omai. Thus the chariot of
Queen Mab, my team of bulls and the crickets, the ark,
the Sphinx, and the balloons, with Hilaro Frosticos, Gog
and Magog, Lord Whittington, and the Lord Mayor's
show, Don Quixote, &c., with my fleet of canoes, alto-
gether cut a very formidable appearance on our arrival
at the Isthmus of Darien. Sensible of what general benefit
it would he to mankind, I immediately formed a plan of
cutting a canal across the isthmus from sea to sea.

For this purpose I drove my chariot with the greatest impetuosity repeatedly from shore to shore, in the
same track, tearing up the rocks and earth thereby, and
forming a tolerable bed for the water. Gog and Magog
next advanced at the head of a million of people from the
realms of North and South America, and from Europe,
and with infinite labour cleared away the earth, &c., that
I had ploughed up with my chariot. I then again drove my
chariot, making the canal wider and deeper, and ordered
Gog and Magog to repeat their labour as before. The canal being a quarter of a mile broad, and three hundred
yards in depth, I thought it sufficient, and immediately
let in the waters of the sea. I did imagine, that from the
rotatory motion of the earth on its axis from west to east
the sea would be higher on the eastern than the western
coast, and that on the uniting of the two seas there would

be a strong current from the east, and it happened just as I expected. The sea came in with tremendous magnificence, and enlarged the bounds of the canal, so as to make a passage of some mile broad from ocean to ocean, and make an island of South America. Several sail of trading vessels and men-of-war sailed through this new channel to the South Seas, China, &c., and saluted me with all their cannon as they passed.

I looked through my telescope at the moon, and perceived the philosophers there in great commotion. They could plainly discern the alteration on the surface of our globe, and thought themselves somehow interested in the enterprise of their fellow-mortals in a neighbouring planet. They seemed to think it admirable that such little beings as we men should attempt so magnificent a performance, that would be observable even in a separate world.

Thus having wedded the Atlantic Ocean to the South Sea, I returned to England, and found Wauwau precisely in the very spot whence she had set out, after having led us a chase all round the world.

CHAPTER XXXIII

*The Baron goes to Petersburgh, and converses with the Em-
press—Persuades the Russians and Turks to cease cutting one
another's throats, and in concert cut a canal across the Isthmus
of Suez—The Baron discovers the Alexandrine Library, and
meets with Hermes Trismegistus—Besieges Seringapatam, and
challenges Tippoo Sahib to single combat—They fight—The
Baron receives some wounds on his face, but at last vanquishes
the tyrant—The Baron returns to Europe, and raises the hull of
the Royal George.*

SEIZED WITH A FURY OF CANAL-CUTTING, I
took it in my head to form an immediate communication between the Mediterranean and the Red Sea, and
therefore set out for Petersburgh.

The sanguinary ambition of the Empress would not
listen to my proposals, until I took a private opportunity,
taking a cup of coffee with her Majesty, to tell her that I
would absolutely sacrifice myself for the general good
of mankind, and if she would accede to my proposals,
would, on the completion of the canal, *ipso facto,* give her
my hand in marriage!

"My dear, dear Baron," said she, "I accede to everything you please, and agree to make peace with the Porte

on the conditions you mention. And," added she, rising with all the majesty of the Czarina, Empress of half the world, "be it known to all subjects, that We ordain these conditions, for such is our royal will and pleasure."

I now proceeded to the Isthmus of Suez, at the head of a million of Russian pioneers, and there united my forces with a million of Turks, armed with shovels and pickaxes. They did not come to cut each other's throats, but for their mutual interest, to facilitate commerce and civilisation, and pour all the wealth of India by a new channel into Europe. "My brave fellows," said I, "consider the immense labour of the Chinese to build their celebrated wall; think of what superior benefit to mankind is our present undertaking; persevere, and fortune will second your endeavours. Remember it is Munchausen who leads you on, and be convinced of success."

Saying these words, I drove my chariot with all my might in my former track, that vestige mentioned by the Baron de Tott, and when I was advanced considerably, I felt my chariot sinking under me. I attempted to drive on, but the ground, or rather immense vault, giving way, my chariot and all went down precipitately. Stunned by the fall, I was some moments before I could recollect myself, when at length, to my amazement, I perceived myself fallen into the Alexandrine Library, overwhelmed in an ocean of books; thousands of volumes came tumbling on my head amidst the ruins of that part of the vault through which my chariot had descended, and for a time buried my bulls and all beneath a heap of learning. However, I contrived to extricate myself, and advanced with awful admiration through the vast avenues of the library. I perceived on every side innumerable volumes and repositories of ancient learning, and all the science of the Antediluvian world. Here I met with Hermes Trismegistus, and a parcel of old philosophers debating upon the politics and learning of their days. I gave them inexpressible delight in telling them, in a few words, all the discoveries of Newton, and the history of the world since their time. These gentry, on the contrary, told me a thousand stories of antiquity that some of our antiquarians would give their very eyes to hear.

In short, I ordered the library to be preserved, and I intend making a present of it, as soon as it arrives in England, to the Royal Society, together with Hermes Trismegistus, and half a dozen old philosophers. I have got a beautiful cage made, in which I keep these extraordinary creatures, and feed them with bread and honey, as they seem to believe in a kind of doctrine of transmigration, and will not touch flesh. Hermes Trismegistus especially is a most antique looking being, with a beard half a yard long, covered with a robe of golden embroidery, and prates like a parrot. He will cut a very brilliant figure in the Museum.

Having made a track with my chariot from sea to sea, I ordered my Turks and Russians to begin, and in a few hours we had the pleasure of seeing a fleet of British East Indiamen in full sail through the canal. The officers of this fleet were very polite, and paid me every applause and congratulation my exploits could merit. They told me of their affairs in India, and the ferocity of that dreadful warrior, Tippoo Sahib, on which I resolved to go to India and encounter the tyrant. I travelled down the Red Sea to Madras, and at the head of a few Sepoys and Europeans pursued the flying army of Tippoo to the gates of

Seringapatam. I challenged him to mortal combat, and, mounted on my steed, rode up to the walls of the fortress amidst a storm of shells and cannon-balls. As fast as the bombs and cannon-balls came upon me, I caught them in my hands like so many pebbles, and throwing them against the fortress, demolished the strongest ramparts of the place. I took my mark so direct, that whenever I aimed a cannon-ball or a shell at any person on the ramparts I was sure to hit him: and one time perceiving a tremendous piece of artillery pointed against me, and knowing the ball must be so great it would certainly stun me, I took a small cannon-ball, and just as I perceived the engineer going to order them to fire, and opening his mouth to give the word of command, I took aim and drove my ball precisely down his throat.

Tippoo, fearing that all would be lost, that a general and successful storm would ensue if I continued to batter the place, came forth upon his elephant to fight me; I saluted him, and insisted he should fire first.

Tippoo, though a barbarian, was not deficient in politeness, and declined the compliment; upon which I took off my hat, and bowing, told him it was an advantage Munchausen should never be said to accept from so gallant a warrior: on which Tippoo instantly discharged his carbine, the ball from which, hitting my horse's ear, made him plunge with rage and indignation. In return I discharged my pistol at Tippoo, and shot off his turban. He had a small field-piece mounted with him on his elephant, which he then discharged at me, and the grapeshot coming in a shower, rattled in the laurels that covered and shaded me all over, and remained pendant like berries on the branches. I then advancing, took the proboscis of his elephant, and turning it against the rider, struck him repeatedly with the extremity of it on either side of the head, until I at length dismounted him. Nothing could equal the rage of the barbarian finding himself thrown from his elephant. He rose in a fit of despair, and rushed against my steed and myself: but I scorned to fight him at so great a disadvantage on his side, and directly dismounted to fight him hand to hand. Never did I fight with any man who bore himself more nobly than this adversary; he parried my blows, and dealt home his own in return with astonishing precision. The first blow of his sabre I received upon the bridge of my nose, and but for the bony firmness of that part of my face, it would have descended to my mouth. I still bear the mark upon my nose.

He next made a furious blow at my head, but I, parrying, deadened the force of his sabre, so that I received but one scar on my forehead, and at the same instant, by a blow of my sword, cut off his arm, and his hand and sabre fell to the earth; he tottered for some paces, and dropped at the foot of his elephant. That sagacious animal, seeing the danger of his master, endeavoured to protect him by flourishing his proboscis round the head of the Sultan.

Fearless I advanced against the elephant, desirous to take alive the haughty Tippoo Sahib; but he drew a pistol from his belt, and discharged it full in my face as I rushed upon him, which did me no further harm than wound my cheek-bone, which disfigures me somewhat under my left eye. I could not withstand the rage and impulse of that moment, and with one blow of my sword separated his head from his body.

I returned overland from India to Europe with

admirable velocity, so that the account of Tippoo's defeat by me has not as yet arrived by the ordinary passage, nor can you expect to hear of it for a considerable time. I simply relate the encounter as it happened between the Sultan and me; and if there be any one who doubts the truth of what I say, he is an infidel, and I will fight him at any time and place, and with any weapon he pleases.

Hearing so many persons talk about raising the Royal George, I began to take pity on that fine old ruin of British plank, and determined to have her up. I was sensible of the failure of the various means hitherto employed for the purpose, and therefore inclined to try a method different from any before attempted. I got an immense balloon, made of the thickest sail-cloth, and having descended in my diving-bell, and properly secured the hull with enormous cables, I ascended to the surface, and fastened my cables to the balloon. Prodigious multitudes were assembled to behold the elevation of the Royal George, and as soon as I began to fill my balloon with inflammable air the vessel evidently began to move: but when my balloon was completely filled, she carried up the Royal George with the greatest rapidity. The vessel appearing on the surface occasioned a universal shout of triumph from the millions assembled on the occasion. Still the balloon continued ascending, trailing the hull after like a lantern at the tail of a kite, and in a few minutes appeared floating among the clouds.

It was then the opinion of many philosophers that it would be more difficult to get her down than it had been to draw her up. But I convinced them to the contrary by taking my aim so exactly with a twelve-pounder, that I brought her down in an instant.

I considered, that if I should break the balloon with a cannon-ball while she remained with the vessel over the land, the fall would inevitably occasion the destruction of the hull, and which, in its fall, might crush some of the multitude; therefore I thought it safer to take my aim when the balloon was over the sea, and pointing my twelve-pounder, drove the ball right through the balloon, on which the inflammable air rushed out with great force, and the Royal George descended like a falling star into the very spot from whence she had been taken. There she still remains, and I have convinced all Europe of the possibility of taking her up.

CHAPTER XXXIV

The Baron makes a speech to the National Assembly, and drives out all the members—Routs the fishwomen and the National Guards—Pursues the whole rout into a Church, where he defeats the National Assembly, &c., with Rousseau, Voltaire, and Beelzebub at their head, and liberates Marie Antoinette and the Royal Family.

PASSING THROUGH SWITZERLAND ON MY return from India, I was informed that several of the German nobility had been deprived of the honours and immunities of their French estates. I heard of the sufferings of the amiable Marie Antoinette, and swore to avenge every look that had threatened her with insult. I went to the cavern of these Anthropophagi, assembled to debate, and gracefully patting the hilt of my sword to my lips—"I swear," cried I, "by the sacred cross of my sword, that if you do not instantly reinstate your king and his nobility, and your injured queen, I will cut the one half of you to pieces."

On which the President, taking up a leaden inkstand, flung it at my head. I stooped to avoid the blow, and rushing to the tribunal seized the Speaker, who was fulminating against the Aristocrats, and taking the creature by one leg, flung him at the President. I laid about me most nobly, drove them all out of the house, and locking the doors put the key in my pocket.

I then went to the poor king, and making my obeisance to him—"Sire," said I, "your enemies have all fled. I alone am the National Assembly at present, and I shall register your edicts to recall the princes and the nobility; and in future, if your majesty pleases, I will be your Parliament and Council." He thanked me, and the amiable Marie Antoinette, smiling, gave me her hand to kiss.

At that moment I perceived a party of the National Assembly, who had rallied with the National Guards, and a vast procession of fishwomen, advancing against me. I deposited their Majesties in a place of safety, and with my drawn sword advanced against my foes. Three hundred fishwomen, with bushes dressed with ribbons in their hands, came hallooing and roaring against me like so many furies. I scorned to defile my sword with their blood, but seized the first that came up, and making her kneel down I knighted her with my sword, which so terrified the rest that they all set up a frightful yell and ran away as fast as they could for fear of being aristocrated by knighthood.

As to the National Guards and the rest of the Assembly, I soon put them to flight; and having made prisoners of some of them, compelled them to take down their national, and put the old royal cockade in its place.

I then pursued the enemy to the top of a hill, where a most noble edifice dazzled my sight; noble and sacred it was, but now converted to the vilest purposes, their monument *de grands hommes,* a Christian church that these Saracens had perverted into abomination. I burst open

the doors, and entered sword in hand. Here I observed all the National Assembly marching round a great altar erected to Voltaire; there was his statue in triumph, and the fishwomen with garlands decking it, and singing "Ca ira!" I could bear the sight no longer; but rushed upon these pagans, and sacrificed them by dozens on the spot. The members of the Assembly, and the fishwomen, continued to invoke their great Voltaire, and all their masters in this monument *de grands hommes*, imploring them to come down and succour them against the Aristocrats and the sword of Munchausen. Their cries were horrible, like the shrieks of witches and enchanters versed in magic and the black art, while the thunder growled, and storms shook the battlements, and Rousseau, Voltaire, and Beelzebub appeared, three horrible spectres; one all meagre, mere skin and bone, and cadaverous, seemed death, that hideous skeleton; it was Voltaire, and in his hand were a lyre and a dagger. On the other side was Rousseau, with a chalice of sweet poison in his hand, and between them was their father Beelzebub!

I shuddered at the sight, and with all the enthusiasm of rage, horror, and piety, rushed in among them. I seized that cursed skeleton Voltaire, and soon compelled him to renounce all the errors he had advanced; and while he spoke the words, as if by magic charm, the whole assembly shrieked, and their pandemonium began to tumble in hideous ruin on their heads.

I returned in triumph to the palace, where the Queen rushed into my arms, weeping tenderly. "Ah, thou flower of nobility," cried she, "were all the nobles of France like thee, we should never have been brought to this!"

I bade the lovely creature dry her eyes, and with the

King and Dauphin ascend my carriage, and drive post to
Mont-Medi, as not an instant was to be lost. They took
my advice and drove away. I conveyed them within a few
miles of Mont-Medi, when the King, thanking me for
my assistance, hoped I would not trouble myself any farther, as he was then, he presumed, out of danger; and
the Queen also, with tears in her eyes, thanked me on
her knees, and presented the Dauphin for my blessing.
In short, I left the King eating a mutton chop. I advised
him not to delay, or he would certainly be taken, and
setting spurs to my horse, wished them a good evening,
and returned to England. If the King remained too long
at table, and was taken, it was not my fault.

AFTERWORD

BY THOMAS SECCOMBE

It is a curious fact that of that class of literature to which Munchausen belongs, that namely of *Voyages Imaginaires*, the three great types should have all been created in England. Utopia, Robinson Crusoe, and Gulliver, illustrating respectively the philosophical, the edifying, and the satirical type of fictitious travel, were all written in England, and at the end of the eighteenth century a fourth type, the fantastically mendacious, was evolved in this country. Of this type Munchausen was the modern original, and remains the classical example. The adaptability of such a species of composition to local and topical uses might well be considered prejudicial to its chances of obtaining a permanent place in literature. Yet Munchausen has undoubtedly achieved such a place. The Baron's notoriety is universal, his character proverbial, and his name as familiar as that of Mr. Lemuel Gulliver, or Robinson Crusoe, mariner, of York. Condemned by the learned, like some other masterpieces, as worthless, Munchausen's travels have obtained such a world-wide fame, that the story of their origin possesses a general and historic interest apart from whatever of obscurity or of curiosity it may have to recommend it.

The work first appeared in London in the course of the year 1785. No copy of the first edition appears to be accessible; it seems, however, to have been issued some time in the autumn, and in the *Critical Review* for December 1785 there is the following notice: "Baron Munchausen's Narrative of his Marvellous Travels and Campaigns in Russia. Small 8vo, 1s. (Smith). This is a satirical production calculated to throw ridicule on the bold assertions of some parliamentary declaimers. If rant may be best foiled at its own weapons, the author's design is not ill-founded; for the marvellous has never been carried to a more whimsical and ludicrous extent." The reviewer had probably read the work through from one paper cover to the other. It was in fact too short to bore the most blasé of his kind, consisting of but forty-nine small octavo pages. The second edition, which is in the British Museum, bears the following title: "Baron Munchausen's Narrative of his Marvellous Travels and Campaigns in Russia; humbly dedicated and recommended to country gentlemen, and if they please to be repeated as their own after a hunt, at horse races, in watering places, and other such polite assemblies; round the bottle and fireside. Smith. Printed at Oxford. 1786." The fact that this little pamphlet again consists of but forty-nine small octavo pages, combined with the similarity of title (as far as that of the first edition is given in the *Critical Review*), publisher, and price, affords a strong presumption that it was identical with the first edition. This edition contains only chapters ii., iii., iv., v., and vi. (pp. 10–44) of the present reprint. These chapters are the best in the book and their substantial if peculiar merit can hardly be denied, but the pamphlet appears to have met with little success,

and early in 1786 Smith seems to have sold the property
to another bookseller, Kearsley. Kearsley had it enlarged,
but not, we are expressly informed, in the preface to the
seventh edition, by the hand of the original author (who
happened to be in Cornwall at the time). He also had it
illustrated and brought it out in the same year in book
form at the enhanced price of two shillings, under the
title:

"Gulliver Revived: The Singular Travels, Campaigns,
Voyages and Sporting Adventures of Baron Munnikhou-
son commonly pronounced Munchausen; as he relates
them over a bottle when surrounded by his friends. A
new edition considerably enlarged with views from the
Baron's drawings. London. 1786." A well-informed *Critical Reviewer* would have amended the title thus: "Lucian
reviv'd: or Gulliver Beat with his own Bow."

Four editions now succeeded each other with rapidity
and without modification. A German translation appeared in 1786 with the imprint London: it was, however,
in reality printed by Dieterich at Göttingen. It was a free
rendering of the fifth edition, the preface being a clumsy
combination of that prefixed to the original edition with
that which Kearsley had added to the third.

The fifth edition (which is, with the exception of
trifling differences on the title-page, identical with the
third, fourth, and sixth) is also that which has been followed in the present reprint down to the conclusion of
chapter twenty, where it ends with the words "the great
quadrangle." The supplement treating of Munchausen's
extraordinary flight on the back of an eagle over France to
Gibraltar, South and North America, the Polar Regions,
and back to England is derived from the seventh edition

of 1793, which has a new sub-title:—"Gulliver reviv'd, or the Vice of Lying properly exposed." The preface to this enlarged edition also informs the reader that the last four editions had met with extraordinary success, and that the supplementary chapters, all, that is, with the exception of chapters ii., iii., iv., v., and vi., which are ascribed to Baron Munchausen himself, were the production of another pen, written, however, in the Baron's manner. To the same ingenious person the public was indebted for the engravings with which the book was embellished. The seventh was the last edition by which the classic text of Munchausen was seriously modified. Even before this important consummation had been arrived at, a sequel, which was within a fraction as long as the original work (it occupies pp. 163–299 of this volume), had appeared under the title, "A Sequel to the Adventures of Baron Munchausen. . . . Humbly dedicated to Mr. Bruce the Abyssinian traveller, as the Baron conceives that it may be some service to him, previous to his making another journey into Abyssinia. But if this advice does not delight Mr. Bruce, the Baron is willing to fight him on any terms he pleases." This work was issued separately. London, 1792, 8vo.

Such is the history of the book during the first eight or constructive years of its existence, beyond which it is unnecessary to trace it, until at least we have touched upon the long-vexed question of its authorship.

Munchausen's travels have in fact been ascribed to as many different hands as those of Odysseus. But (as in most other respects) it differs from the more ancient fabulous narrative in that its authorship has been the subject of but little controversy. Many people have entertained

erroneous notions as to its authorship, which they have
circulated with complete assurance; but they have not
felt it incumbent upon them to support their own views
or to combat those of other people. It has, moreover,
been frequently stated with equal confidence and inac-
curacy that the authorship has never been settled. An
early and persistent version of the genesis of the travels
was that they took their origin from the rivalry in fabulous tales of three accomplished students at Göttingen
University, Bürger, Kästner, and Lichtenberg; another
ran that Gottfried August Burger, the German poet and
author of "Lenore," had at a later stage of his career met
Baron Munchausen in Pyrmont and taken down the
stories from his own lips. Percy in his anecdotes attri-
butes the Travels to a certain Mr. M. (Munchausen also
began with an M.) who was imprisoned at Paris during
the Reign of Terror. Southey in his "Omniana" conjectured, from the coincidences between two of the tales
and two in a Portuguese periodical published in 1730,
that the English fictions must have been derived from
the Portuguese. William West the bookseller and numerous followers have stated that Munchausen owed its first
origin to Bruce's Travels, and was written for the purpose
of burlesquing that unfairly treated work. Pierer boldly
stated that it was a successful anonymous satire upon
the English government of the day, while Meusel with
equal temerity affirmed in his "Lexikon" that the book
was a translation of the "well-known Munchausen lies"
executed from a (non-existent) German original by Rudolph Erich Raspe. A writer in the *Gentleman's Magazine*
for 1856 calls the book the joint production of Bürger and
Raspe.

Of all the conjectures, of which these are but a selection, the most accurate from a German point of view is that the book was the work of Bürger, who was the first to dress the Travels in a German garb, and was for a long time almost universally credited with the sole proprietorship. Bürger himself appears neither to have claimed nor disclaimed the distinction. There is, however, no doubt whatever that the book first appeared in English in 1785, and that Bürger's German version did not see the light until 1786. The first German edition (though in reality printed at Göttingen) bore the imprint London, and was stated to be derived from an English source; but this was, reasonably enough, held to be merely a measure of precaution in case the actual Baron Munchausen (who was a well-known personage in Göttingen) should be stupid enough to feel aggrieved at being made the butt of a gross caricature. In this way the discrepancy of dates mentioned above might easily have been obscured, and Bürger might still have been credited with a work which has proved a better protection against oblivion than "Lenore," had it not been for the officious sensitiveness of his self-appointed biographer, Karl von Reinhard. Reinhard, in an answer to an attack made upon his hero for bringing out Munchausen as a pot-boiler in German and English simultaneously, definitely stated in the *Berlin Gesellschafters* of November 1824, that the real author of the original work was that disreputable genius, Rudolph Erich Raspe, and that the German work was merely a free translation made by Bürger from the fifth edition of the English work. Bürger, he stated, was well aware of, but was too high-minded to disclose the real authorship.

Taking Reinhard's solemn asseveration in conjunc-
tion with the ascertained facts of Raspe's career, his
undoubted acquaintance with the Baron Munchausen
of real life and the first appearance of the work in 1785,
when Raspe was certainly in England, there seems to be
little difficulty in accepting his authorship as a positive
fact. There is no difficulty whatever, in crediting Raspe
with a sufficient mastery of English idiom to have written the book without assistance, for as early as January
1780 (since which date Raspe had resided uninterrupt-
edly in this country) Walpole wrote to his friend Mason
that "Raspe writes English much above ill and speaks it
as readily as French," and shortly afterwards he remarked
that he wrote English "surprisingly well." In the next year,
1781, Raspe's absolute command of the two languages
encouraged him to publish two moderately good prose-
translations, one of Lessing's "Nathan the Wise," and the
other of Zachariae's Mock-heroic, "Tabby in Elysium."
The erratic character of the punctuation may be said, with
perfect impartiality, to be the only distinguishing feature
of the style of the original edition of "Munchausen."

Curious as is this long history of literary misappro-
priation, the chequered career of the rightful author,
Rudolph Erich Raspe, offers a chapter in biography
which has quite as many points of singularity.

Born in Hanover in 1737, Raspe studied at the Universities of Göttingen and Leipsic. He is stated also to have
rendered some assistance to a young nobleman in sow-
ing his wild oats, a sequel to his university course which
may possibly help to explain his subsequent aberrations.
The connection cannot have lasted long, as in 1762, having already obtained reputation as a student of natural

history and antiquities, he obtained a post as one of the clerks in the University Library at Hanover.

No later than the following year contributions written in elegant Latin are to be found attached to his name in the Leipsic *Nova Acta Eruditorum*. In 1764 he alluded gracefully to the connection between Hanover and England in a piece upon the birthday of Queen Charlotte, and having been promoted secretary of the University Library at Gottingen, the young savant commenced a translation of Leibniz's philosophical works which was issued in Latin and French after the original MSS. in the Royal Library at Hanover, with a preface by Raspe's old college friend Kästner (Göttingen, 1765). At once a courtier, an antiquary, and a philosopher, Raspe next sought to display his vocation for polite letters, by publishing an ambitious allegorical poem of the age of chivalry, entitled "Hermin and Gunilde," which was not only exceedingly well reviewed, but received the honour of a parody entitled " Harlequin and Columbine." He also wrote translations of several of the poems of Ossian, and a disquisition upon their genuineness; and then with better inspiration he wrote a considerable treatise on "Percy's Reliques of Ancient Poetry," with metrical translations, being thus the first to call the attention of Germany to these admirable poems, which were afterwards so successfully ransacked by Bürger, Herder, and other early German romanticists.

In 1767 Raspe was again advanced by being appointed Professor at the Collegium Carolinum in Cassel, and keeper of the landgrave of Hesse's rich and curious collection of antique gems and medals. He was shortly afterwards appointed Librarian in the same city, and in 1771 he married. He continued writing on natural history, mineralogy, and archaeology, and in 1769 a paper in the 59th volume of the Philosophical Transactions, on the bones and teeth of elephants and other animals found in North America and various boreal regions of the world, procured his election as an honorary member of the Royal Society of London. His conclusion in this paper that large elephants or mammoths must have previously existed in boreal regions has, of course, been abundantly justified by later investigations. When it is added that Raspe during this part of his life also wrote papers on lithography and upon musical instruments, and translated Algarotti's Treatise on "Architecture, Painting, and Opera Music," enough will have been said to make manifest his very remarkable and somewhat prolix versatility. In 1773 he made a tour in Westphalia in quest of MSS., and on his return, by way of completing his education, he turned journalist, and commenced a periodical called the *Cassel Spectator*, with Mauvillon as his co-editor. In 1775 he was travelling in Italy on a commission to collect articles of vertu for the landgrave, and it was apparently soon after his return that he began appropriating to his own use valuable coins abstracted from the cabinets entrusted to his care. He had no difficulty in finding a market for the antiques which he wished to dispose of, and which, it has been charitably suggested, he had every intention of replacing whenever opportunity should serve. His consequent procedure was, it is true, scarcely that of a hardened criminal. Having obtained the permission of the landgrave to visit Berlin, he sent the keys of his cabinet back to the authorities at Cassel—and disappeared. His thefts, to the amount of two thousand rixdollars, were promptly discovered, and advertisements were issued for the arrest of the Councillor Raspe, described without suspicion of flattery as a long-faced man, with small eyes, crooked nose, red hair under a stumpy peri-wig, and a jerky gait. The necessities that prompted him to commit a felony are possibly indicated by the addition that he usually appeared in a scarlet dress embroidered with gold, but sometimes in black, blue, or grey clothes. He was seized when he had got no farther than Klausthal, in the Hartz mountains, but he lost no time in escaping from the clutches of the police, and made his way to England. He never again set foot on the continent.

He was already an excellent English scholar, so that when he reached London it was not unnatural that he should look to authorship for support. Without loss of time, he published in London in 1776 a volume on some German Volcanoes and their productions; in 1777 he translated the then highly esteemed mineralogical travels of Ferber in Italy and Hungary. In 1780 we have an inter-esting account of him from Horace Walpole, who wrote to his friend, the Rev. William Mason: "There is a Dutch sa-vant come over who is author of several pieces so learned that I do not even know their titles: but he has made a discovery in my way which you may be sure I believe, for it proves what I expected and hinted in my 'Anecdotes of Painting,' that the use of oil colours was known long before Van Eyck." Raspe, he went on to say, had discov-ered a MS. of Theophilus, a German monk in the fourth century, who gave receipts for preparing the colours, and had thereby convicted Vasari of error. "Raspe is poor, and I shall try and get subscriptions to enable him to print his work, which is sensible, clear, and unpretend-ing." Three months later it was, "Poor Raspe is arrested by his tailor. I have sent him a little money, and he hopes to recover his liberty, but I question whether he will be able to struggle on here." His "Essay on the Origin of Oil Painting" was actually published through Walpole's good service in April 1781. He seems to have had plans of going to America and of excavating antiquities in Egypt, where he might have done good service, but the bad name that he had earned dogged him to London. The Royal Society struck him off its rolls, and in revenge he is said to have threatened to publish a travesty of their transactions. He was doubtless often hard put to it for a living, but the variety of his attainments served him in good stead. He possessed or gained some reputation as a mining expert, and making his way down into Cornwall, he seems for some years subsequent to 1782 to have been assay-master and storekeeper of some mines at Dolcoath. While still at Dolcoath, it is very probable that he put together the little pamphlet which appeared in London at the close of 1785, with the title "Baron Munchausen's Narrative of his Marvellous Travels and Campaigns in Russia," and having given his *jeu d'esprit* to the world, and possibly earned a few guineas by it, it is not likely that he gave much further thought to the matter. In the course of 1785 or 1786, he entered upon a task of much greater magnitude and immediate importance, namely, a descriptive catalogue of the Collection of Pastes and Impressions from Ancient and Modern Gems, formed by James Tassie, the eminent connoisseur. Tassie engaged Raspe in 1785 to take charge of his cabinets, and to commence describing their contents: he can hardly have been ignorant of his employee's delinquencies in the past, but he probably estimated that mere casts of gems would not offer sufficient temptation to a man of Raspe's eclectic tastes to make the experiment a dangerous one. Early in 1786, Raspe produced a brief but well-executed conspectus of the arrangement and classification of the collection, and this was followed in 1791 by "A Descriptive Catalogue," in which over fifteen thousand casts of ancient and modern engraved gems, cameos, and intaglios from the most renowned cabinets in Europe were enumerated and described in French and English. The two quarto volumes are a monument of patient and highly skilled industry, and they still fetch high prices. The elaborate introduction prefixed to the work was dated from Edinburgh, April 16, 1790.

This laborious task completed, Raspe lost no time in applying himself with renewed energy to mineralogical work. It was announced in the *Scots Magazine* for October 1791 that he had discovered in the extreme north of Scotland, where he had been invited to search for minerals, copper, lead, iron, manganese, and other valuable products of a similar character.

From Sutherland he brought specimens of the finest clay, and reported a fine vein of heavy spar and "every symptom of coal." But in Caithness lay the loadstone which had brought Raspe to Scotland. This was no other than Sir John Sinclair of Ulbster, a benevolent gentleman of an ingenious and inquiring disposition, who was anxious to exploit the supposed mineral wealth of his barren Scottish possessions. With him Raspe took up his abode for a considerable time at his spray-beaten castle on the Pentland Firth, and there is a tradition, among members of the family, of Sir John's unfailing appreciation of the wide intelligence and facetious humour of Raspe's conversation. Sinclair had some years previously discovered a small vein of yellow mundick on the moor of Skinnet, four miles from Thurso. The Cornish miners he consulted told him that the mundick was itself of no value, but a good sign of the proximity of other valuable minerals. Mundick, said they, was a good horseman, and always rode on a good load. He now employed Raspe to examine the ground, not designing to mine it himself, but to let it out to other capitalists in return for a royalty, should the investigation justify his hopes. The necessary funds were put at Raspe's disposal, and masses of a bright, heavy material were brought to Thurso Castle as a foretaste of what was coming. But when the time came for the fruition of this golden promise, Raspe disappeared, and subsequent inquiries revealed the deplorable fact that these opulent ores had been carefully imported by the mining expert from Cornwall, and planted in the places where they were found. Sir Walter Scott must have had the incident (though not Raspe) in his mind when he created the Dousterswivel of his "Antiquary." As for Raspe, he betook himself to a remote part of the United Kingdom, and had commenced some mining operations in county Donegal, when he was carried off by scarlet fever at Muckross in 1794. Such in brief outline was the career of Rudolph Erich Raspe, scholar, swindler, and undoubted creator of Baron Munchausen.

The merit of Munchausen, as the adult reader will readily perceive, does not reside in its literary style, for Raspe is no exception to the rule that a man never has a style worthy of the name in a language that he did not prattle in. But it is equally obvious that the real and original Munchausen, as Raspe conceived and doubtless intended at one time to develop him, was a delightful

personage whom it would be the height of absurdity to
designate a mere liar. Unfortunately the task was taken
out of his hand and a good character spoiled, like many
another, by mere sequel-mongers. Raspe was an impudent scoundrel, and fortunately so; his impudence
relieves us of any difficulty in resolving the question, —to
whom (if any one) did he owe the original conception of
the character whose fame is now so universal.

When Raspe was resident in Göttingen he obtained,
in all probability through Gerlach Adolph von Munchausen, the great patron of arts and letters and of Göttingen
University, an introduction to Hieronynimus Karl Friedrich von Munchausen, at whose hospitable mansion at
Bodenwerder he became an occasional visitor. Hieronynimus, who was born at Bodenwerder on May 11, 1720,
was a cadet of what was known as the black line of the
house of Rinteln Bodenwerder, and in his youth served
as a page in the service of Prince Anton Ulrich of Brunswick. When quite a stripling he obtained a cornetcy in
the "Brunswick Regiment" in the Russian service, and
on November 27, 1740, he was created a lieutenant by letters patent of the Empress Anna, and served two arduous
campaigns against the Turks during the following years.
In 1750 he was promoted to be a captain of cuirassiers by
the Empress Elizabeth, and about 1760 he retired from
the Russian service to live upon his patrimonial estate at
Bodenwerder in the congenial society of his wife and his
paragon among huntsmen, Rösemeyer, for whose particular benefit he maintained a fine pack of hounds. He kept
open house, and loved to divert his guests with stories,
not in the braggart vein of Dugald Dalgetty, but so embellished with palpably extravagant lies as to crack with a

humour that was all their own. The manner has been appropriated by Artemus Ward and Mark Twain, but it was invented by Munchausen. Now the stories mainly relate to sporting adventures, and it has been asserted by one contemporary of the baron that Munchausen contracted the habit of drawing such a long-bow as a measure of self-defence against his invaluable but loquacious henchman, the worthy Rösemeyer. But it is more probable, as is hinted in the first preface, that Munchausen, being a shrewd man, found the practice a sovereign specific against bores and all other kinds of serious or irrelevant people, while it naturally endeared him to the friends of whom he had no small number.

He told his stories with imperturbable *sang froid*, in a dry manner, and with perfect naturalness and simplicity. He spoke as a man of the world, without circumlocution; his adventures were numerous and perhaps singular, but only such as might have been expected to happen to a man of so much experience. A smile never traversed his face as he related the least credible of his tales, which the less intimate of his acquaintance began in time to think he meant to be taken seriously. In short, so strangely entertaining were both manner and matter of his narratives, that "Munchausen's Stories" became a by-word among a host of appreciative acquaintance. Among these was Raspe, who years afterwards, when he was starving in London, bethought himself of the incomparable baron. He half remembered some of his sporting stories, and supplemented these by gleanings from his own commonplace book. The result is a curious medley, which testifies clearly to learning and wit, and also to the turning over of musty old books of *facetiæ* written in execrable Latin.

The story of the Baron's horse being cut in two by the descending portcullis of a besieged town, and the horseman's innocence of the fact until, upon reaching a fountain in the midst of the city, the insatiate thirst of the animal betrayed his deficiency in hind quarters, was probably derived by Raspe from the *Facetiæ Bebelianæ* of Heinrich Bebel, first published at Strassburgh in 1508.

There it is given as follows: "De Insigni Mendacio. Faber clavicularius quem superius fabrum mendaciorum dixi, narravit se terapore belli, credens suos se subsecuturos equitando ad cujusdam oppidi portas penetrasse: et cum ad portas venisset cataractam turre demissam, equum suum post ephippium discidisse, dimidiatumque reliquisse, atque se media parte equi ad forum usque oppidi equitasse, et caedem non modicam peregisse. Sed cum retrocedere vellet multitudine hostium obrutus, tum demum equum cecidisse seque captum fuisse."

The drinking at the fountain was probably an embellishment of Raspe's own. Many of Bebel's jests were repeated in J. P. Lange's *Deliciæ Academicæ* (Heilbronn, 1665), a section of which was expressly devoted to "Mendacia Ridicula"; but the yarn itself is probably much older than either. Similarly, the quaint legend of the thawing of the horn was told by Castiglione in his *Cortegiano*, first published in 1528. This is how Castiglione tells it: A merchant of Lucca had travelled to Poland in order to buy furs; but as there was at that time a war with Muscovy, from which country the

furs were procured, the Lucchese merchant was
directed to the confines of the two countries. On
reaching the Borysthenes, which divided Poland
and Muscovy, he found that the Muscovite traders remained on their own side of the river from
distrust, on account of the state of hostilities. The
Muscovites, desirous of being heard across the
river, announced the prices of their furs in a loud
voice; but the cold was so intense that their words
were frozen in the air before they could reach the
opposite side. Hereupon the Poles lighted a fire in
the middle of the river, which was frozen into a
solid mass; and in the course of an hour the words
which had been frozen up were melted, and fell
gently upon the further bank, although the Muscovite traders had already gone away. The prices
demanded were, however, so high that the Lucchese merchant returned without making any
purchase. A similar idea is utilised by Kabelais
in *Pantagruel*, and by Steele in one of his *Tatlers*.
The story of the cherry tree growing out of the
stag's head, again, is given in Lange's book, and
the fact that all three tales are of great antiquity
is proved by the appearance of counterparts to
them in Lady Guest's edition of the *Mabinogion*.
A great number of *nugae canorae* of a perfectly
similar type are narrated in the sixteenth century
"Travels of the Finkenritter" attributed to Lorenz
von Lauterbach.

To humorous waifs of this description, without fixed
origin or birthplace, did Kaspe give a classical setting

amongst embroidered versions of the baron's sporting jokes. The unscrupulous manner in which he affixed Munchausen's own name to the completed *jeu d'esprit* is, ethically speaking, the least pardonable of his crimes; for when Raspe's little book was first transformed and enlarged, and then translated into German, the genial old baron found himself the victim of an unmerciful caricature, and without a rag of concealment. It is consequently not surprising to hear that he became soured and reticent before his death at Bodenwerder in 1797.

Strangers had already begun to come down to the place in the hope of getting a glimpse of the eccentric nobleman, and foolish stories were told of his thundering out his lies with apoplectic visage, his eyes starting out of his head, and perspiration beading his forehead. The fountain of his reminiscences was in reality quite dried up, and it must be admitted that this excellent old man had only too good reason to consider himself an injured person.

In this way, then, came to be written the first delightful chapters of Baron Munchausen's "Narrative of his Travels and Campaigns in Russia." It was not primarily intended as a satire, nor was it specially designed to take off the extravagant flights of contemporary travellers. It was rather a literary frivolity, thrown off at one effort by a tatterdemalion genius in sore need of a few guineas.

The remainder of the book is a melancholy example of the fallacy of enlargements and of sequels. Neither Raspe nor the baron can be seriously held responsible for a single word of it. It must have been written by a bookseller's hack, whom it is now quite impossible to identify, but who was evidently of native origin; and the

book is a characteristically English product, full of personal and political satire, with just a twang of edification.
The first continuation (chapters one and seven, to twenty,
inclusive), which was supplied with the third edition, is
merely a modern *rechauffé*, with "up to date" allusions, of
Lucian's *Vera Historia*. Prototypes of the majority of the
stories may either be found in Lucian or in the twenty
volumes of *Voyages Imaginaires*, published at Paris in
1787. In case, however, any reader should be sceptical as
to the accuracy of this statement he will have no very
great difficulty in supposing, as Dr. Johnson supposed
of Ossian, that anybody could write a great amount of
such stuff if he would only consent to abandon his mind
to the task.

With the supplementary chapters commence topical allusions to the recently issued memoirs of Baron
de Tott, an enterprising Frenchman who had served the
Great Turk against the Russians in the Crimea (an English translation of his book had appeared in 1785). The
satire upon this gallant soldier's veracity appears to be
quite undeserved, though one can hardly read portions
of his adventures without being forcibly reminded of the
Baron's laconic style. It is needless to add that the amazing account of De Tott's origin is grossly libellous. The
amount of public interest excited by the aeronautical exploits of Montgolfier and Blanchard was also playfully
satirised. Their first imitator in England, Vincenzo Lu-
nardi, had made a successful ascent from Moorfields as
recently as 1784, while in the following year Blanchard
crossed the channel in a balloon and earned the sobriquet
Don Quixote de la Manche. His grotesque appropriation
of the motto "*Sic itur ad astra*" made him, at least, a fit

object for Munchausen's gibes. In the Baron's visit to Gibraltar we have evidence that the anonymous writer, in common with the rest of the reading public, had been studying John Drinkwater's "History of the Siege of Gibraltar" (completed in 1783), which had with extreme rapidity established its reputation as a military classic. Similarly, in the Polar adventures, the "Voyage towards the North Pole," 1774, of Constantine John Phipps, afterwards Lord Mulgrave, is gently ridiculed, and so also some incidents from Patrick Brydone's "Tour through Sicily and Malta" (1773), are, for no obvious reason, contemptuously dragged in. The exploitation of absurd and libellous chapbook lives of Pope Clement XIV., the famous Ganganelli, can only be described as a low bid for vulgar applause. A French translation of Baron Friedrich von Trenck's celebrated Memoirs appeared at Metz in 1787, and it would certainly seem that in overlooking them the compiler of Munchausen was guilty of a grave omission. He may, however, have regarded Trenck's adventures less as material for ridicule than as a series of *hâbleries* which threatened to rival his own.

The Seventh Edition, published in 1793, with the supplement (pp. 142–161), was, with the abominable proclivity to edification which marked the publisher of the period (that of "Goody Two-Shoes" and "Sandford and Merton"), styled "Gulliver Reviv'd: *or the Vice of Lying Properly Exposed.*" The previous year had witnessed the first appearance of the sequel, of which the full title has already been given, "with twenty capital copperplates, including the baron's portrait." The merit of Munchausen as a mouthpiece for ridiculing traveller's tall-talk, or indeed anything that shocked the incredulity of the age, was by this time widely recognised. And hence with some little ingenuity the popular character was pressed into the service of the vulgar clamour against James Bruce, whose "Travels to Discover the Sources of the Nile" had appeared in 1790. In particular Bruce's description of the Abyssinian custom of feeding upon "live bulls and kava" provoked a chorus of incredulity. The traveller was ridiculed upon the stage as Macfable, and in a cloud of ephemeral productions; nor is the following allusion in Peter Pindar obscure:—

"Nor have I been where men (what loss alas!)
Kill half a cow, then send the rest to grass."

The way in which Bruce resented the popular scepticism is illustrated by the following anecdote told by Sir Francis Head, his biographer. A gentleman once observed, at a country house where Bruce was staying, that it was not possible that the natives of Abyssinia could eat raw meat! "Bruce said not a word, but leaving the room, shortly returned from the kitchen with a piece of raw beef-steak, peppered and salted in the Abyssinian fashion. 'You will eat that, sir, or fight me', he said. When the gentleman had eaten up the raw flesh (most willingly would he have eaten his words instead), Bruce calmly observed, 'Now, sir, you will never again say it is *impossible*'." In reality, Bruce seems to have been treated with much the same injustice as Herodotus. The truth of the bulk of his narrative has been fully established, although a passion for the picturesque may certainly have led him to embellish

many of the minor particulars. And it must be remembered, that his book was not dictated until twelve years
after the events narrated.

Apart from Bruce, however, the sequel, like the previous continuation, contains a great variety of political,
literary, and other allusions of the most purely topical
character Dr. Johnson's Tour in the Hebrides, Mr. Pitt,
Burke's famous pamphlet upon the French Revolution,
Captain Cook, Tippoo Sahib (who had been brought to
bay by Lord Cornwallis between 1790 and 1792). The rev-
olutionary pandemonium in Paris, and the royal flight to
Varennes in June 1791, and the loss of the "Royal George"
in 1782, all form the subjects of quizzical comments, and
there are many other allusions the interest of which is
quite as ephemeral as those of a Drury Lane pantomime
or a Gaiety Burlesque.

Nevertheless the accretions have proved powerless
to spoil "Munchausen." The nucleus supplied by Raspe
was instinct with so much energy that it has succeeded
in vitalising the whole mass of extraneous extravagance.

Although, like "Gulliver's Travels," "Munchausen"
might at first sight appear to be ill-suited, in more than
one respect, for the nursery, yet it has proved the delight
of children of all ages; and there are probably few, in the
background of whose childish imagination the astonishing Munchausen has not at one time or another, together
with Robinson Crusoe, Jack-the-Giant-Killer, and the
Pied Piper of Hamelyn, assumed proportions at once gigantic and seductively picturesque.

The work, as has been shown, assumed its final form
before the close of the eighteenth century; with the nine-
teenth it commenced its triumphant progress over the

civilised world. Some of the subsequent transformations
and migrations of the book are worthy of brief record.

A voluminous German continuation was published
at Stendhal in three volumes between 1794 and 1800.
There was also a continuation comprising exploits at
Walcheren, the Dardanelles, Talavera, Cintra, and else-
where, published in London in 1811. An elaborate French
translation, with embellishments in the French manner,
appeared at Paris in 1862. Immerman's celebrated novel
entitled "Munchausen" was published in four volumes
at Dusseldorf in 1841, and a very free rendering of the
Baron's exploits, styled "Munchausen's Lugenabenteuer,"
at Leipsic in 1846. The work has also been translated into
Dutch, Danish, Magyar (*Bard de Mánx*), Russian, Portuguese, Spanish (*El Conde de las Maravillas*), and many
other tongues, and an estimate that over one hundred
editions have appeared in England, Germany, and America alone, is probably rather under than above the mark.

The book has, moreover, at the same time provided
illustrations to writers and orators, and the richest and
most ample material for illustrations to artists. The original rough woodcuts are anonymous, but the possibilities
of the work were discovered as early as 1809, by Thomas
Rowlandson, who illustrated the edition published in
that year. The edition of 1859 owed embellishments to
Crowquill, while Cruikshank supplied some character-
istic woodcuts to that of 1869. Coloured designs for the
travels were executed by a French artist Richard in 1878,
and illustrations were undertaken independently for
the German editions by Riepenhausen and Hosemann
respectively. The German artist Adolph Schrödter has
also painted a celebrated picture representing the Baron

surrounded by his listeners. But of all the illustrations yet invented, the general verdict has hitherto declared in favour of those supplied to Théophile Gautier's French edition of 1862 by Gustave Doré, who fully maintained by them the reputation he had gained for work of a similar genre in his drawings for Balzac's *Contes Drôlatiques*. When, however, the public has had an opportunity of appreciating the admirably fantastic drawings made by Mr. William Strang and Mr. J. B. Clark for the present edition, they will probably admit that Baron Munchausen's indebtedness to his illustrators, already very great, has been more than doubled.